Girls Drive Jeeps

By

Candace Meredith

ISBN: 978-1-914130-80-9

Girls Drive Jeeps – Candace Meredith

4

Dedicated to my three children who inspire me to write and to my loyal partner who without him life would feel incomplete.

OTHER TITLES BY IMPSPIRED

Stolen –
by Candace Meredith

Hometown -
by Ken Cathers

The Kingdom –
by Mary Farrell

A Snowfall in Paris -
by Theresa C. Gaynord

Snakes and a Broken Ladder –
by Steve Cawte

A Bell in the Morning –
by Kevin McManus

Poetland –
by Henry Bladon

Preface

When Tamara Day met Blakely O'Connor it was the turn of a new decade. That's when they were newly thirteen and I was sixteen. Blakely, my sister, got rides from her big sister – that's me, Vanessa O'Connor, and this is Blakely's story. The one story that I know. The story she would tell if she wasn't being modest. Blakely and Tamara were best friends. They did everything together, and at the end of this story there is a lesson, and I'm going to tell it from the beginning.

Chapter One

Class had started. Blakely casually opened her notebook and began to pencil her name when the table adjacent to her erupted with young female banter.

"You're ugly," the frail blonde said from across the room.

Blakely looked up from her notebook to find a timid, beautiful girl sitting in front of her turning away from the blonde and the brunette.

"Don't let her talk to you like that," Blakely said with an attitude, but Tamara was startled.

"Shut up!" Blakely scolded the blonde and turned to Tamara. "Seriously, don't let them talk to you like that."

"You don't have to defend me," Tamara's voice cracked.

"They told me the same thing. That I was ugly. Just yesterday. Don't pay them any attention – you're not ugly."

Blakely had this thing where she could stick up for others, but she couldn't stick up for herself – she was too shy and the fearful type. She found her strength when sticking up for the underdog. Tamara was taken aback. No one had ever stood up for her before. With the passing of each day, in literature class, as they sat facing one another at a table made of four desks all pushed together, Tamara and Blakely's bond grew, and they had an affinity for each other. By the middle of seventh grade, Tamara and Blakely were known to hold hands, sit in one another's lap at the lunch table, and be otherwise inseparable. Blakely wasn't exploring her sexuality at that age, but she loved Tamara and Tamara loved her back. They were best friends, and as close as anyone could get. Blakely began wearing makeup in junior high and the boys noticed her. Tamara joined her at the mirror and together they coated their lashes with the darkest noir. Our father did not approve. This was the time of our parents' divorce, when Blakely and I stayed with our father to finish out the school year. Blakely became rebellious after a shady upbringing with a mother who seemed to cherish her moments with alcohol and boyfriends over time with her daughters. Our father didn't know how to handle Blakely. Blakely was not interested in obeying. She took her makeup to school and wore showy clothing. My sister came to me for advice about how to get away from Dad's strict policies, but I wasn't much help back then. I had my first boyfriend and I had a Jeep. It was red. I was a fiery and fierce redhead behind the wheel of my own ride. My very first ride. I, too, went wild. The first place I took my sister was on a trip to a theme park where roller coasters and rides abound for the wild child at heart. Blakely and Tamara got to ride in the back seat while I drove with the top down and Adam, my boyfriend, gloated in the passenger seat.

11

"I'm riding shotgun with all these hotties," he said.

Tamara and Blakely blushed. He was sweet to her and her friends. To others, we looked like an open pack of Skittles: our hair was vibrant hues of red (mine), jet black (Blakely), and dirty blonde (Tamara). Adam's was auburn and he decided to grow a goatee. Adam Hardt was still a teen, too, just turned nineteen, and Dad was unsure about him. But he was athletic and played ball at the local technical school. I was in my junior year of high school and would be turning seventeen in June. That's when school would end and Blakely would turn fourteen in July. The theme park was a three-hour drive from home. Back then, during our parents' divorce, it was usual for my sister to be in my car. I took her everywhere; our mother was usually absent. It wasn't that she didn't love us – she did. She worked hard, but she played even harder. She worked long hours as a cocktail waitress, then stayed after hours at the casinos. She loved to drink. The party was our demise and her pastime. She left our father. Dad didn't know how to handle us, especially with Blakely's first period – that is, when again, I came in. I broke it all down for her casually. She listened. Life was full of things they don't necessarily teach in biology class, but should.

School was out. Our birthdays were pending – another month and then two. We enjoyed our close birthdays. We were close as sisters. Tamara was like a sister, too. The high school girls began to treat them differently; they wanted them as friends. They wanted their energy and their passion. They asked why they held hands in the halls; they didn't care – they answered simply *because she's my best friend.* They meant it. Tamara's brothers, Tommy and Shane, often took care of their sister the way I took care of Blakely. Tommy was the oldest, aged twenty-four, and Shane was only a year older than Tamara. Shane adored Blakely, and I realize now that Tamara was jealous of that, too. Tamara lived in a one-bedroom house with her bedroom being a walk-through to her parents' room. They, too, were in the middle of a divorce. Her mother was taken to another man. Her family was broken, and they were cared for by a lonely father. I realized later that Tamara needed the bond of a woman, which she found in Blakely. Her mother was absent, too. I get it. But not all endings are happy. I will carefully, casually, break the news. But there's a story with a beautiful past, too. So, I'll start with that. When, during Tamara's folks' divorce, they began to party, how they became popular, how they went to senior week, and how, when it came crashing down, they were left with their faces to the rain. Not talking. This is a story about love, hate, and love again. This is a story about friendship and loss.

School let out officially on June 5th when we weren't skipping. Blakely had her yearbook signed by her junior high friends. The pages were filled. She and Tamara gained popularity among them, but they all were to be divided between two counties; there were those to attend Bell High School and others Stanton High. Blakely was to attend Bell and Tamara to attend Stanton. But Blakely was quick-witted; she forged an out-of-district form by our seldom seen and absent mother. I told her it would never work but then she begged me to take her to school, just until she got some wheels of her own, and I caved. I gave in to that poor plight of a girl who didn't have a mother. Dad was dating by the summer. He found the mother of a friend who was named Alisa; her daughter, Samira, was Blakely's friend. A friend after the fact. After Blakely stopped taking crap from other girls, she gained Samira's respect. Samira had lush, long eyelashes, and a body to die for. She had always been popular with the boys. She had long wavy hair and dark skin; she was a mixed girl, and had the best of both worlds. She was in Blakely and Tamara's boat; her parents were divorced. Our father met her mother at the local laundromat. Dad was repairing some washing machine parts, a side job he kept as a mechanic, when Samira's mother tripped over his tool belt. Dad found her pretty. She was elegant in work clothes, having come home from the job to find her washer broken. Dad said he could fix that, too. He showed up with dinner and flowers. She was impressed. He fixed her washer, whatever was broken, and he fixed her broken life. Alisa's husband, Samira's father, was hard core and determined. Alisa grew tired and wanted to live a little. Take the edge off with someone less severe and that's where Dad was good. Michael Allen O'Connor was calm and relaxed; too chill for a mother who wanted to party. Samira grew to like Dad; she called him Mr. Mike and later *my second dad*, though he wouldn't become her stepdad for five years. Alisa was beautiful and strong. She was thin and taller than most women at six feet with slender long legs and a

14

perfectly flat stomach. Dad was six-foot-one and they saw
eye-to-eye. Alisa was well-kempt and worked in sales;
she was a service writer for a high-end car dealer. She
sold Porsches, Bentleys and Volvos. She dabbled in real
estate, and her first sale was a million bucks. She had
money. Dad had talent; eventually, he would build their
first home with his own hands. Alisa had an eye for nice
things and decorated well. Blakely and I would be out of
high school by then, but Samira and Blakely would at
times forget their relations and let out a slip-of-the-
tongue. *She's always spending money,* Blakely said once,
and Samira slit her eyes and Tamara sighed. They did,
back then, have one another's back. Back then. That's
when things were normal. It was normal for Blakely to sit
between Tamara's legs on an amusement ride because it
was summer and the local carnival had come to town.

It was the summer of the new millennium when
Blakely wore her cut-off shorts and hoodie despite the
ninety-degree temperature. She'd rather sweat than not
look cute. Tamara was more practical in a tank. The boys
wanted Blakely; Tamara would slit her own eyes then.
Blakely would flirt. She had a perfect tummy and a full
body; she bloomed early. Tamara took her by the hand
and they went to the Gravitron where another girl would
puke. They lost their appetite and found funnel cake
looked eerily similar. They laughed. I told them I'd pick
them up at nine … it was only seven, and I spotted them
from the Ferris wheel. Adam rolled his eyes.

"At least she's not letting them hang out," he said,
and I slapped the back of his head.

"What?" he said and then laughed.

My sister was full-figured and very beautiful. I liked it better when she was shyer, less heavy on the makeup. When it was less cause for concern in the way of boys. But back then, before her lashing-out at the girl, Kennedy, who called them ugly, she was practically suicidal; the girls at her school were brutal. Back then it was a struggle. I was in high school and couldn't always defend her – she needed to find her own way. And she did. She found her voice the day they called Tamara ugly.

The carnival was a teen's outlet from school. They rode rides that made them dizzy. When the nausea wore off, they ate pizza and shared a cola. It was hot. It was summer and in three months they would enter high school, but Blakely hadn't broken the news to Tamara yet. Tamara was a poor farm girl who lived in a three-room shack and Blakely and I didn't fare too well beyond that. We lived in a modest house with three bedrooms, one bath, and old wooden floors that showed the marks since 1937 when it was built. It's another reason Tamara and Blakely lived on love. They had each other. I had Adam, but Blakely also had me. I had Blakely too, but Adam loved her as if she were his own little sister. The four of us had each other, even if she was younger. Tamara's brothers were always on her side, too. When the hatred grew, they kept their distance. The tables turned and it seemed nothing would be the same anymore. Tamara met Alisa and Samira – she told us no one could replace her love for her own father, but Dad was right up there on her list of people to buy gifts for Christmas. When things went south, so did Tamara's love for the family The gist is in the beginning of these pages. The rest is the story and the end is hard, rough, rugged and raw (even complex) emotion. Time is all that can heal the pain, and time is not kind, and life can be unfair and unjust. I'll tell the story and let you decide.

Chapter Two

"Come here, Tamara," Blakely said when she placed a folded piece of paper in her hand. They were out by the lake at the watershed enjoying the view. The watershed was walking distance from the house. They sat before a picturesque blue sky. Tamara unfolded the paper and read what it said: Blakely would be attending Stanton High School. Tamara took a deep breath and when she exhaled, Blakely could smell the sweet cinnamon on her breath. *Even her breath is sweet*, Blakely thought, and she hugged her around the neck. Tamara marveled and they smiled together to celebrate the continuation of their seeing one another every day. They walked a mile down the road to the dam, a refuge they would use often for late night parties, and gatherings around a place they lovingly called *The Rock*. A place where boys would bring alcohol and hold their girlfriends in their arms the way Tamara would hold Blakely. They passed by the dam and entered the woods where they would sit by the reservoir, the place where there would be many bonfires and sipping on *forties* of malt liquor. I can't say I condone underage drinking, because I don't, but this is once again Blakely's story and it is for her that I want to tell it with an open and earnest heart. Blakely and I didn't have a mother who was still at home and Dad was busy. He left sometimes for weeks when he took up a new job as a semi-truck driver. It paid better, but the hours were sometimes long and strenuous. Dad was kinda a jack-of-all trades and dabbled in many jobs. Alisa enjoyed his versatility. He, too, enjoyed her well-rounded attributes. On the outside they looked odd and possibly not like a couple, but Dad was built strong and our genes made us handsome. He was a looker and so was she – but their attire was off. Dad wore flannels and jeans; Alisa was classy and elegant, and mostly wore skirts and heels. *The Odd Couple*, we heard more than once, but Dad was happy. Samira was Blakely's age, in the same grade, but Samira would live with her father to stay in the Bell High School community. We would only see Samira on weekends, and she had another class of friends; they were a clique – not the party type but more *preppy* and into cheerleading. Blakely and I had never been in the cheer squad. Blakely played lacrosse and I played volleyball and tennis. We were active, semi-athletic, but good at what we did while in high school. Eventually lacrosse wasn't as important as the parties, but Blakely knew that lacrosse was temporary, and friendships were for life.

Tamara dabbled her toes in the water; the summer heat permeated the landscape. The water was cool and the minnows bit at their ankles – they laughed. Tamara broke the news that her dad was losing the farm and that she needed to get a job – if she could help him in any way, she would. She was one hundred percent a daddy's girl and she loathed seeing him in pain.

"Where will you work?" Blakely asked with a frown.

"I won't be too busy, don't worry, but I'm going

19

to turn in my application at the local restaurant *The Poet's Corner.*"

"That place is new…"

"Yeah, so they're looking for people…."

"Maybe I can get a job there, too…"

"Do you want to work?"

"I can try." They laughed again.

Blakely put in her application and asked for Dad's signature for the work release program. They were still only thirteen, but they got their first jobs at the newest restaurant in town. Blakely worked as a hostess and Tamara took on a job in the kitchen; her mother loved to cook and taught her all that she knew. *The Poet's Corner* was an artsy kind of place that served a great menu of vegan, Italian and Asian inspired food, eclectic and fascinating for a restaurant. They served an open buffet on Friday nights when Blakely worked the dining room and Tamara worked the front coffee bar, known as a trucker stop, and they primarily worked weekends, aside from Tuesday night when Blakely filled in as hostess for a single mom who couldn't work that night anymore. I primarily drove the girls to work, and I had a job in retail at the souvenir shop. I worked as a cashier initially until a year later when they promoted me to shop manager. Blakely would be promoted to waitress at age fifteen and Tamara would continue to cook, but until then they worked three nights a week and after their shifts ended, they found rides and went out to the reservoir where they had a fire and more.

Back at the reservoir, before the parties, the girls enjoyed watching the fishermen in the boats when they heard from behind the boisterous voices of men – teens who wanted to cast their line from the shore. There was a tone of excitement in their voices. Blakely looked casually over her shoulder to catch a glimpse of a young man wearing navy blue swimming trunks who waded in the water – swimming wasn't allowed at the reservoir – but they didn't appear to follow the rules. *Chadwick*, one of them called loudly. *Stop calling me that!* He bellowed before becoming submerged in the water. The reservoir was warm like bath water. The air temperature was at nearly one hundred, and Blakely thought how nice it would be to go for a swim. Tamara kept her back to the boys. She was clearly not interested. Blakely wondered if Chadwick had a real name. The other boys were still laughing; Chadwick, or whatever his name was, was out in the deep almost. He began to holler that he was sharing the water with a beaver. Then Blakely watched as he climbed the rock formation on the opposite side; he stood tall at what she thought was a height above six feet and his brown skin glistened like he'd been oiled in self-tanner. He faded out of view then re-appeared over the rock-wall edge and he jumped – he jumped from the wall and became submerged. Then his head bobbed above the surface. Chadwick floated on his back and Blakely wondered if the boys had noticed them sitting there at all when one of them took a few steps in their direction.

21

"Sorry if we're being loud," he said, "we don't mean to interrupt your good time or anything."

Blakely thought he was being sincere. Tamara thought they were being assholes.

"We don't mind," Blakely said back in her most honest voice.

"Don't lead them on…" Tamara wanted no justification that they were slightly amused. Blakely's hair blew in a soft breeze and Tamara smelled essence of lavender shampoo; she huffed, "It smells so good." She bit her lip. "But those guys," she nudged.

"I don't mind them," Blakely flashed her a smile. Tamara rolled her eyes.

Blakely turned her head again to find Chadwick emerging from the water – walking toward them – he looked like a tall, lean, brown golden god. At closer range she could tell he was a native, or a mixed ethnicity like Samira, and Blakely, oddly, felt a hint of jealously in the pit of her stomach; she didn't want him to have that in common with someone she knew could be her stepsister. He was gorgeous, she thought at that moment. His hair was cut high and shaved on the sides but long on top and pulled into a hair band. He had tattoos on both biceps and his legs were strong with muscular definition and his stomach, a washboard – Blakely did not know how Tamara could not be in love too.

"Oh god, he's coming," Tamara said under her

22

breath.

"He's…" Blakely wanted to say gorgeous, but stifled her tongue.

"You should get in the water," he told them, and smiled, showing perfect white teeth. She smiled back. He, they, were older. They were my age and older. Around nineteen. Blakely was crushed, she confessed later. Tamara took her by the hand, and they put their feet in the water; Tamara turned her face to the sun. They got wet to their knees. The girls giggled and the boys took their tackle – apparently, they weren't really there to fish – and went away like the bright sun. At night Dad built a fire. Blakely said she was leaving with a friend.

"Who are you going with?" I said.

"Relax," Blakely said. "It's Tommy picking us up. I'm going to Tamara's."

That night Blakely dreamed about Chadwick, wishing she had gotten a real name.

In the morning the girls were awoken by the sound of the rooster. Tamara was used to it. Blakely sighed and turned over wishing she'd sleep a little longer. Tamara got out of bed promptly as she did every morning, but this time she dragged a sleepy Blakely along to feed the goats. One new mother drank happily as the baby drank from her under belly. A mother cow also approached the fence to get a look at the new girl when Blakely also noticed her calf; the baby was on wobbly

23

legs.

"She was born overnight," Tamara said.

"She's so cute," Blakely smiled and ducked beneath the fence rail to get a better look.

"Do you want to name her?" Tamara finished with the feed and opened the fence gate to allow Blakely closer to the new calf.

"Do they go to the slaughterhouse?" She was timid.

"No, we just have milk cows on our farm." Tamara was proud to see Blakely cheer up and pet the calf.

"I like Violet or Charlotte." She was earnest.

"It's Violet, then." Tamara went on to the pigs with some slop.

Blakely had stopped mentioning the boys from the day before after Tamara told her, "They're too old, anyway."

She was right.

The girls showered and dressed after the feeding was finished and Tamara fixed a brunch. She poured lemonade and made biscuits with jam and some sausage gravy. Tamara wanted to be a chef and someday open her own restaurant, so she practiced being in the kitchen. She

24

cut peppers and made omelets for her brothers who were
due in any minute. They spent their mornings bailing hay
and manning the farm equipment. Tamara told Blakely
how her mother taught her to cook by the age of eleven,
and then she watched cooking shows to improve her
style; working at *The Poet's Corner* was a perfect job for
Tamara. She intended to go to culinary art school at the
major art institute in the neighboring town. Blakely was
okay with her start at the restaurant as a hostess and felt
that she could continue serving tables through college.
Blakely wanted to attend veterinary school and the
experience on Tamara's parents' farm was perfect as well.
As soon as she had the thought, Tamara's two older
brothers entered the kitchen and washed their hands
before being served a slightly later breakfast.

"Sorry, it's late," Tamara laughed. "It was hard
getting Blakely out of bed."

Blakely grimaced.

Their father, Thomas Scott Day, and his sons
Tommy Junior and Shane Andrew Day, were into their
meal when Tamara asked a question.

"Do you think I can go to Blakely's tonight?"
Tamara was innocent. That was the beginning of the girls
falsifying they were staying at one another's house when
in fact they would be going to the pool hall with girls
who were already sixteen. The girls did look older than
their age, but they were yet to turn fourteen – Tamara
four weeks after Blakely – and they often acted beyond

their age. Tamara's mother, Bonnie, had moved out of the house and had a new boyfriend who Tamara was yet to meet; Bonnie was ten years younger than Thomas and the boys shamed her for leaving their father. Tamara also would not be leaving her father.

"I reckon you can stay at Blakely's tonight," her father had said. He didn't look up from the table; he chewed slowly and casually took a sip of homemade lemonade. Blakely got a to-go cup for herself. She was fond of her friend's old-fashioned cooking. The girls went out the door; the screen was busted, and the farm was muddy. It rained the day before. Blakely didn't want to get her new shoes dirty and grimaced when the brothers came out after them.

"Look here little lady," Tommy said with a twang, and he lifted her off her feet and put her down in the gravel. Blakely laughed. Tamara rolled her eyes. She was possessive of her friend and wanted her brothers to flirt with her less. The girls heard of a bonfire going on that night and asked if they could have a ride to Blakely's house and of course I obliged. I helped my little sister to get home and they went off into her room. They blared the music and chatted by the open window over who was going to be at the party.

The party was scheduled at *The Rock*. That's where the girls would be walking – at the end of our street they'd hang a right and end up at the watershed where they'd cross over the rock formations, past the overlook and next to the reservoir.

26

They arrived at nine. The party wasn't a disappointment. There were cars and Jeeps stationed at the now-closed location, but there was no blockage to the access points. They were secluded there, and no one would typically bother them. The party involved anyone from a freshman to a senior – they just had their cliques. Tamara knew of the party through Tommy, and she knew most of the boys there because they were friends of her brother. The boys looked out for Tamara and wouldn't dare to bother them. The kids hanging out were of the Stanton school district and Blakely would only know a handful of the girls who went to grade school together – they were a band of girls whose parents let them do anything. Like Dad, unwittingly. Like Thomas. Tamara also knew a handful of country girls whose twang reminded Blakely of her brothers. Tamara sang too; she sounded like one of the Dixie Girls and had a bell-like voice; she hit the high notes in a deeply pitched accent. She was country but a little bit of pop. When the girls were invited to tailgate, they found the trail that led back to the road and there they met some girls who would also be entering Stanton for their freshman year.

Cherish was one of the girls, and her best friend was Lacy. Cherish grew up in a military family and traveled a lot but had been in the same area for the past four years. Lacy was her best friend from grade school and they both would be attending Stanton as freshmen. Lacy was quiet with dark skin and lean with beautiful lines, like the angular shape of her jaw and hair extensions; Cherish was rather her opposite with olive skin, jade-colored eyes, lashes to die for, but kind of dark.

She wrote music, sang like a bell, and had an affinity for horror. Lacy was sweet and preferred a good old romantic comedy. They got along like sisters because of their equal interest in books. They devoured classics and had a penchant for avant-garde that was timeless and witty – Cherish introduced the dark comedy to Lacy who marveled over the dark ones who had superpowers. Tamara sang like a Dixie in their presence, and they opened Pandora's Box with that one; they relished in one another's life story. Like a good book. Blakely could hold a note, too, and the four of them became a symphony of class and charm. Cherish, alongside Lacy, both took pity on the poor farm girl who sang *Take Me Home* like a country chick who was high on life – and she was; although penniless, she had Blakely. With four singing beauties, the others crowded around the tailgating party while dishing out wine coolers. The boys doted on the girls, but Tamara kept Blakely in her reach; she wasn't going to allow them to swarm her like fish do a pebble. Blakely folded her small frame into Tamara's lap and they perched there with beer can in hand and the teenage dreamers partied with the sound of music and cheap beer. They tossed each other into the water and sat by the fire in the night of a June sky – they were young. And school was out of session. They all had each other, and their folks' leniency wouldn't get past the local police in due time. Some of their favorite hangouts were the parking lots and one of them was a small church with a stream and a pond where Blakely would sit beside the water with Tamara and they would chat about work while hanging out. But on this night, they didn't talk about work; they listened instead to Cherish and Lacy chat about where they worked. They worked at the golf resort over the summer where they managed the concession stands, and they gloated about the tips they made and how many high rollers – in the way of money – would flirt with them.

"I met a boy named Jason," Cherish said as she drank a peach flavored beverage and giggled like a schoolgirl. She had already turned fourteen in February. Lacy turned fourteen a week before in May. Being fourteen had an appeal like crossing the threshold of truly being a teenage kid. Like they were way past the whole just-became-a-teenager stage.

"What's Jason like?" Blakely asked as the music died.

"He's gorgeous. And seventeen. He can totally drive his dad's car."

The others laughed.

"His dad has a Jag," Lacy inferred and Cherish continued.

"He'll have his own ride soon. He sold his truck."

She talked about Jason's love of hot rides, how he fixed them up, worked in his brother's shop as a body mechanic, and was going to own his pair of wheels if he could convince his dad he wouldn't smash it.

"He had it all jacked up," Cherish said flatly,

29

implying his truck had a lift kit. Jason's brother Mike had a body shop, and they were in need of a receptionist, the other girl there, Skye Laney, piped in.

"I need to apply if he has any hot friends," she winked.

"Totally," Cherish chimed. A song came across the radio and the girls began to sing again but Skye, like myself, couldn't hold a note. They became known as *the girls by the river* to the local police and on that night the police never showed, and the reservoir became a refuge for the local teens who wanted to drink because time was idling by and they didn't want to miss a thing.

Chapter Three

Mom and Dad got along only for the occasion of a party. Mom wouldn't talk to Alisa – she was immature like that. But for the sake of my seventeenth birthday, she kept her cool. The party was at Dad's house, our mom's house when it had been the home they started together, but Alisa had already put her stamp on it; the décor was in her own style – retro and chic. She wore bell-bottoms, and Mom preferred stilettos. Dad didn't have a type. He married them solely out of attraction for different sets of qualities. Adam brought the cake. Blakely decorated along with Tamara. I had a huge sweet sixteen – turning seventeen was even bigger, but we did it in the form of a cook out; we had Maryland blue crabs, corn-on-the-cob, and burgers on the grill. The guests brought potluck dishes. Dad said Mom looked engaged with another guy who was not Steve. Mom wasn't on his good list. Steve was Mom's second husband, and our stepfather. They wed in Vegas. We didn't know. They were very silent.

"It was only three months ago," Dad overheard her say, as he couldn't help but to pry. She was looking extra sharp despite the occasion – skinny jeans and heels. The guy she was talking to, Allen, was a neighbor of many years. Dad suspected she had been cheating years ago and assumed Allen was her accomplice. Allen seemed genuine, but Blakely and I assumed he didn't date women. Then Steve showed moments later; he was cut like a wrestler and liked beer. Dad didn't do beer. The guests brought their own beverages. The teens were forbidden to drink. Dad had his limitations, but we knew there'd be an after party.

"Donna, you're looking sharp," Adam had everyone's attention, "what's the occasion?"

The rest of us were proper in flops and visors.

"Adam, you're so loud," Mom gushed.

Mom had no reason or excuse. She just liked fashion and any occasion to her was reasonable to put on the spiky heels.

We learned that Mom stayed on a yacht for her honeymoon, and Steve owned a resort and a golfing business. He said they were looking for a receptionist and asked if I was interested in a summer job. Blakely realized he owned the resort the girls talked about the night before. That made Blakely uncomfortable – she didn't want Mom knowing her friends, at least not that closely. Dad never gave her credit, but Mom had a way of knowing someone deeply and intimately without an iota of sex. Mom had her way of getting to know the juicy details of one's relationship – she suspected Tamara and Blakely often, but their friendship was simple because of their age.

"I fell in love at thirteen," Mom told her when she was trying to pry.

Blakely rolled her eyes.

Adam then announced it was time to swim. That summer we had an in-ground pool and there was an adult party going on in the pool – Blakely and Tamara opted out in the moment, saying they preferred the heat. Then he did the unthinkable – the DJ showed up. I didn't expect live music but then he asked Tamara to sing. She obliged. She had the voice of pixie dust – if fairies were real they'd sing like a bell, and that was Tamara. She started with a twang in her voice and then she did a softer a cappella and sang her own song. She wrote music to pass the time. Her song was about being alone in the country – a song of survival. She was a little lost without Bonnie, but her brothers helped her keep it together. She wrote about being a daddy's girl and how momma left them alone. Dad seemed solemn. Like it made him think. He wanted to be close to us, but his work drove him harder still. Mom wanted the high life, and he knew she found that, too. He was happiest in Alisa's embrace. She saved him from being a wreck his whole life. Dad was suicidal when Mom left. He felt discontentment with the two of us seeing him that way. His depression mixed with insanity didn't make Mom bat an eye. She was just kind of selfish. Blakely would never sing about that. She would sing about friendships. She was the optimist. I was ready to duck beneath the bench when Dad whispered in her ear – then Tamara led the chorus on wishing me a happy birthday. I was so embarrassed. Adam laughed. I punched his rib cage. They served cake. They went all out. Alisa looked happy serving portions to the guests. Mom talked fashion with Allen who had a penchant for interior design – Mom wanted new curtains. Steve had a trophy for a wife. Mom faired that well in life. She could pass for not a day over thirty. Mom was forty-nine. Dad was fifty-five and Alisa, to Mom's dismay, nine years younger. Mom didn't need to work, not with having Steve, but she ran the books and catalogued the complaints. She'd come at the employees with suspicion and dirty looks. No wonder they were short a receptionist. The resort had a casino. Steve was loaded. Dad worked hard. They were both happy. They wanted the same for us. Blakely and I were on the same page of happiness – they were proud of that. We were two young women, fairing well, whose grades were not bad.

Then Adam took the mic. I groaned. In my reverie I thought of the day we met at the homecoming dance; he was with Michelle Clancy. She was crowned Homecoming Queen. Our school did that – it wasn't just for prom. Then they broke up over tacos. He walked out. She threatened to beat my face in. I hid behind the table and got laughed at. I wasn't one into breaking bad in the cafeteria. She left the school when her parents moved to another state. Adam asked a friend of a friend about that girl with the long sparkling black gown – the one I borrowed from Mom's closet on last notice – and I was her. He tracked me down with a friend in the passenger seat of his Honda Civic. He had ground-effects and some other kind of motor. He loved being under the hood of a car. I got my Jeep at my sweet sixteen – after putting away into savings – and working weekends since I just turned a teen. It was typical to have a job at a young age among our friends. We were not wealthy, and Dad taught us about hard work paying off in the end. Blakely fell in love with a Jeep and a lift kit. "Let's go get this thing stuck," Adam said – the Jeep belonged to his buddy Diesel who everyone called *Big D*. His dad had a warehouse where they worked in lumber, making furniture and rehabbing old houses. Adam was into cars. Diesel was into all the above. His girlfriend, Sherry, my best friend after the day we met, also liked nice rides, and later got a Sahara the color of turquoise. We became the Jeep brigade and Blakely was next to drive one – but she still had to turn fourteen first. Tamara would have to buy her own ride, too – not so much because of learning how to earn it – as Dad had instilled in us – but because they were poor. They were losing the farm, and the farmhouse they were building sat like an empty vessel – a project that was started but would never be finished after Bonnie left for a new man; that new man was Ronald Dalton. Tamara finally broke it to us, and Bonnie was into his music. Ronald worked a second-hand music and book shop, and Bonnie had a crush on his type of vinyl.

Adam broke out in song. I about cried. Then he pulled Blakely in closely and he made her sing along. She looked dumbstruck and awkward, but he bellowed and she laughed. I couldn't help but to fall in love all over again. He really was the best. The party ended that way; with Adam bellowing a loud song. No one could take any more. That night I still heard his words in my head. I dreamed of the day we could live together, then I realized that would be soon; I was entering my senior year and Blakely was beginning high school. We at times felt worlds apart. Blakely entered my room and crashed on my bed. She did that often. Some nights we would stay up and talk over boys and parties; the night would wane to the light of the new day as the moon would settle and the sun peaked over the horizon.

In the light of the morning, Blakely was out of bed. That was the morning Alisa showed us her new ring.

"I didn't want to steal your thunder," she said, and we knew she wanted to wait until the party was over to flash us her new rock; it wasn't quite a rock, but a gem with charisma she said.

"It looks good on your petite finger," Blakely said to her. I could tell that Alisa was liked by Blakely which could be easily accepted after having an absent mother. Donna was like Bonnie in that way – they left our fathers for other men. Tamara likely clung to Blakely for the lack of another woman in her life – the many things to become jealous of. Alisa's ring had a single diamond in the center inset with multitudes of small, studded diamonds that cloaked the center like worker bees to a queen. The ring was beautiful. Exquisite. I wondered if Dad was challenging Mom in some way – Steve was loaded, and Dad had to compare. Or he thought he did. Steve's ownership of the golf resort likely made Dad take his next move to buy some land and plan to build a country inn on it. Blakely was confused.

"Why?" she asked, and Dad just looked at her. Dad and Alisa didn't officially live together yet. He was stuck on home; the house he helped to build from the ground up. He was stuck on it and Alisa didn't think to

36

sell her home, so it was a little twisted that way. Still, they were to get married. And I was happy. It wasn't Dad's fault he was getting married again. Blakely shrugged and went about her business while I sat with Alisa and she talked about Samira.

"She's going to school with you girls," Alisa said, but I didn't break the news that Blakely would be attending Stanton. It didn't occur to either of us to feel bad – but my next thought was Dad finding out now that Samira was going to break the news so I had to cover for my little sis.

"Yeah," I was nonchalant, "Blake is going to Stanton." I was cunning as well. "Because she would die without Tamara."

"When did she do that?" Dad wasn't even offended.

"She asked Mom." Dad totally bought it.

"Oh," he simply said.

I didn't have to mention Blake's forging the letter. And I called her Blake when I felt I was doing something sweet. She knew it too and would ask me what I was up to. When Blakely entered the living room, she looked relieved and I knew she overheard.

"How will she be getting to Stanton?" Alisa was always competent.

"I'll be taking her," I said, and Blakely hugged my

shoulders.

I tossed a pillow at my sister and went outside into the warm day as Blakely followed.

"There's a party tonight," she didn't need to say anymore.

"I'll take you to Tamara's and you'll have to get rides from there."

The plan was set and we both would be seeing our friends that night.

Adam sat in the back seat on his way to Tamara's; he liked the wind in his hair. Blakely turned up the jams to a loud decibel so we couldn't hear her sing – or perhaps she thought. When the song changed to something somber, she turned the radio down.

"I hope Shane and Tommy are there."

I knew it was because they would give them rides. They did as much for Tamara as I did for Blakely. I just smiled knowingly. The parties she attended were typically for sixteen-year-olds, but Tamara and Blakely were ahead of most kids their age. The parties that were for seniors were held separately by grade and by clique and then by school. Adam jumped shotgun when Blakely got out with her bag in tow. She had a thing for Hello Kitty. Adam poked fun but Blakely just rolled her eyes – never to give him the finger. I was surprised. She was usually very expressive. When the front door slammed, we left. We were heading for the parking lot by the Wendy's where we were scheduled to meet, once there we would find the local party.

Most of the fourteen to sixteen crews did not have house parties every Friday night; but on occasion someone left their teenager home alone and the party would be heard about throughout the school. Blakely entered the front door into the kitchen where Shane and Tommy were sitting, having a meal, looking dirty and disheveled.

"Looks like hard work today boys," Blakely said, realizing Tamara was in the shower.

"Who you callin' a boy?" Tommy nudged her shoulder.

"Never touch a lady," Shane slapped him back.

"She ain't no lady."

"She is too!"

"Oh, I know, I'm kidding, come back," he said as Blakely was leaving for Tamara's bedroom – which wasn't a room at all. Her brothers shared the basement while her father had the only bedroom upstairs. The whole house wasn't more than eight hundred square feet. The place Tamara's bed occupied made up the tiny living space; they spent most their time in the kitchen or the basement. Shane was chewing on beef jerky while Tommy poured another glass of Tamara's homemade sweet tea. She was her brothers' best thing. Their mother, Bonnie, showed up in the next ten minutes yielding papers.

"Hello to you too, Mom," Tommy said. As the older brother, he typically led the confrontations.

"Hi, Shane honey," she said and he simply replied with a *hello, Mom.*

"That bitch," Tommy muffled beneath his breath.

Her presence made Blakely feel awkward, especially since Tamara wasn't out of the shower.

"Dad ain't home," Tommy continued.

"Of course he's home, he's a farmer," Bonnie huffed.

Shane peered out the window, got Tommy's attention, and he darted his finger out the window.

"You brought him here?" Tommy shouted, and Blakely began to panic.

"Is that Donald, Mom?" Shane was smooth.

"I know you must…," she was cut off.

"Must know not to bring him here!" Tommy was fuming.

"It's Ronald, sweetie," Bonnie ignored him, "you can call him Ron."

Tommy threw open the door. Shane followed.

"What the fuck are you doing here?" Tommy was livid.

Tamara emerged from the shower to hear the commotion.

"What's going on?" She saw Blakely.

"Your mom is here. And she brought him."

Tamara hadn't met Ronald either. Their mother had left their home quietly and without warning. They hadn't seen their mother for weeks. Thomas was left with two teens, himself being twenty-four years old, and worked the farm for the time being, but Thomas knew he would leave too; Tamara helped as much as she could and tended the goats and prepared them for 4-H. They knew their father needed help on the farm, and they also knew that seeing her new man on his own piece of dirt would tear his heart out.

"Her boyfriend is here?"

"Yeah," Blakely whispered.

Tamara dressed quickly and moved swiftly through the kitchen. She got to the door to hear her mother shouting.

"I told you to stay in the car," her mother said.

"I just want to introduce myself," he said back as

Bonnie moved between them. Tommy was more heated than ever. Bonnie shut the driver side door as Ronald was climbing in.

"Give these to your father," she yielded the papers to Tamara who took them and approached Tommy, whose face grew red and Shane spat chewing tobacco into the dirt.

Blakely emerged from the kitchen as Bonnie peeled away and kicked up dirt. Tamara shuffled through the kitchen.

"They're divorce papers," she said, shaking her head. Blakely sighed.

"I'm sorry," Blakely said softly.

"It's not a big ass deal," Tommy slammed the front door, "but she can't bring him here!"

Shane picked up the bucket of feed off the floor and let the door close softly behind him, and Blakely was relieved to drown out the sound.

Chapter Four

The small two door coupe didn't want to start – Shane's car, the one he called a beater, was hanging on its last limb. No doubt their father scored it from an impound instead of a car lot. It had miles but Shane knew he got it for a couple hundred bucks. Tamara and Blakely piled out of the back of that car while Shane sped off with Tommy in the passenger seat; they had an appointment to sell some farm equipment to a neighbor. Tamara led Blakely down the trail toward the water; in the middle of the woods, thirty teenagers sat in the June heat with alcohol, smokes, and what-else they desired. The girls passed around peach flavored frozen daiquiris the boys scored for them from their older brothers. Blakely cracked open the glass bottle and sipped while they could hear more cars emerging – soon there would be more teens hanging out at *The Rock* where they first got to meet more kids entering Stanton. Tamara broke out a pack of smokes and gave them to a few boys for some cash. Tommy could score her friends some cigarettes. Tamara also drank wine coolers and grabbed Blakely by the hand. They put their arms around one another's shoulders, and Tamara sang some tunes that had been playing in her head since they left the car.

"Your voice is so pretty," another girl said who turned out to be Cherish; she was between the other two girls they had met the other night – Lacy and Skye Davis

43

turned out to be twin sisters; one was just darker than the other and no one would ever guess it. They were bi-racial and very beautiful. Cherish, in dark lipstick, illuminated by the fire, smoked from a pipe. The marijuana was plentiful. They were rebels or just outcasts.

"She's the only one that smokes," Lacy fanned the smoke from her face.

No one would guess too that they were friends. Sometimes strangers were good company and there were facts that opposites attract.

Tamara could finally speak. "Thanks," she said politely.

"No problem," Cherish was richly dark, and Blakely found her fascinating; her hair was an exquisite purple, and her nose was pierced.

"Where did you get that done?" Blakely wanted to break her own tension.

"My brother's a tattoo artist and they do piercings there."

It would be later that Tamara and Blakely got their navels pierced there.

Tamara passed a joint. She never smoked before. She passed it off to a boy who was more than willing who turned out to be Jason.

"Jay-dog," Cherish called him, "don't hog all the

good stuff."

"Puff, puff, pass," his friend Archie Miller said.

"Archie, dude, I'm, ah, give it to you in a minute." He inhaled deeply and held his breath. The scent of pot permeated the landscape and Blakely thought it was a contact buzz.

She sipped her peach flavored wine cooler and listened to the chatter around her – happy that she could break the nervous tension at all.

Tamara tossed the glass into an empty cooler and rummaged for another. She tossed the metal cap into the fire and looked around; there were teens strewn along the nature trail that faded into the dark night where only fires could be seen from the distance. Blakely overheard a conversation to her right.

"This place is going to get busted," one of the boys said.

"Yeah, there's too many heads here tonight," another agreed.

Cherish stood from her spot and moved closer to Jason and Archie.

"Some of us are busting out of here to go to the watershed. Want to go?" She was looking at Tamara and then to Blakely.

"Sure," they looked at one another.

There were ten of them who piled into one large truck; they hid low in the back, but the drive over to the watershed was inconspicuous; the lot was closed at the road so they parked the 4X4 at the street and walked the trail to the reservoir where they would park themselves, and that night they would not build a fire. Instead, the boys would ask the girls if they wanted to go swimming. Blakely was hesitant, but it became no big deal because they were all doing it – and they were doing it together. Blakely and Tamara wiggled out of their jean shorts and tank tops to swim in the reservoir wearing their underclothes. Blakely was glad to have on her favorite silky black underwear and bra beneath her clothes. The girls were the first ones in the water as the guys were still getting undressed. The water was cool, but the June heat was still humid despite the darkness. They bobbed in the water and Blakely enjoyed floating on her back. She had a reverie of Chadwick and his friends from days past. She was interested in getting to know him better, but they didn't exchange numbers. She just wasn't that bold – and she was only thirteen – thinking she wasn't ready for boys. But Tamara held Blakely close and didn't want to see her fall prey to a predator – Tamara's brothers taught her well. Cherish lit a smoke and she was entering the water with the guys. Her boyfriend Jason began to introduce them, "Ladies," he was smooth, "this is my main man Archie here…"

"Yeah, Jase, I think they already know…" Cherish butted in.

"How do they already know?"

46

"We heard the name," Blakely was coy.

"But that's not a formal introduction." Jason touched his hand to his bare chest.

Tamara sunk beneath the water, careful not to get her hair wet, and threw her long, tousled hair into a bun. She reminded Blakely of a Latin singer and Tamara was also fond of the entertainer but didn't see the resemblance. Archie and Jason were among a group of boys who were mostly fifteen to seventeen in age. Those who could drive already had trucks; Blakely liked that. She was a massive truck kind of girl. She loved tailgating parties and *muddin'*. They had only been once, with a group of guys, whose family owned a lot of land; Blakely thought she recognized some of them there. Jason introduced David, Kurt, Joe, and Frankie. Frankie was Italian whose parents came from Italy when he was only three years old. His father learned how to sell life insurance and prospered in the U.S. for his family. Joe's family was from Czech Republic, and they owned a hair salon. Kurt and David were average guys who liked BBQ and were cool with everybody. They loved beer and backyard parties. Cherish and Jason swam to the highest peak and the rest turned to watch them jump. Illuminated by nothing other than the moon, they held hands and jumped from several feet while the rest shouted from the water.

"Want to try it?" David asked the rest of them.

"Sure," Tamara shrugged, and she turned to

Blakely.

"Oh, no, uh-huh, I'm not going up there," Skye's voice was soft and her sister laughed.

"I'm not going up there either," Lacy was the loudest.

Blakely began to swim to the rock formation. David took her by the hand and together the guys, aside from Jason and Blakely and Tamara, climbed onto the rock ledge and once outside the water they could feel the heat permeate their drenched bodies. Archie's other buddy Joe went first. He had long, unkempt hair like a rock singer and he kept it pulled back, fastened with a black band. Then David stood his ground and told them, "Just get a good running start and jump in."

They did just that. Tamara grabbed Blakely's hand and together they left the cliff, and both screamed on their way down. Then the four of them bobbed at the surface like little floating beach balls. Tamara was high on life. She had her best friend, floated on air, and submerged into a pool of warm lava – a liquid of warm love. Blakely was impressed with herself too. She liked Jason and Archie enough, but their friends were super cool, too.

"I heard you have a Jeep," Joe said from above the water.

"It's my sister's," Blakely smiled, and turned to float on her back in the water.

"Oh, okay." Joe seemed to like her, and he was rough looking to Blakely. She liked him, but she would never take it that far.

"How old are you?" he asked.

"I'm thirteen … fourteen next month."

"Cool," Joe said, "I'm fifteen. Sixteen in like six months."

"She's too young for you," Tamara cut in.

Blakely just flashed her a smile. She knew Tamara loved her – but to what extent?

They waded in the water for a while until they swam to catch up with the rest of the crew. Archie was doting over Skye and Blakely learned David and Lacy were a couple. David was thick, muscular, and had bulging biceps. He had dark skin for a Caucasian that he said was permanent all year round for him. His dark skin was paired with darker hair and almond-like eyes. Blakely thought Lacy and David made a nice couple. Skye and Archie seemed to like one another and stayed close in the water. Jason met Cherish in their freshman year, but they didn't hook up until they reconnected over summer. They were both sophomores. Blakely and Tamara felt young compared to them although they were only a year apart. Blakely and Tamara were the only freshmen. In fact, they were all sophomores, so they were indeed the odd ones out. Joe tried to get close to Blakely, but Tamara had no problem coming between them. Blakely and

Tamara were still learning the boundaries of who was coupled with whom, but then there was one girl who they both knew and that was Kennedy – and she brought her own tribe of friends.

"Who is that?" Joe then had his eyes on the brunette.

"That's Jessica," Cherish seemed to be her friend.

Kennedy was a tall and lean blond – a walking cliché. A Barbie. And her friend, Jessica, was a brunette, more brown than red, with blue eyes. They were both pretty. They were accompanied by another girl who was also lean with silk-like black hair, like Blakely's but tapered around her face. Blakely was chic with a strong body and long jet-black hair. Jessica was also short and liked butterflies; she wore necklaces with butterfly pedants that shimmered in gold. Kennedy wore jean shorts and a little red jacket despite the humidity. All the girls were beautiful. Blakely thought the black-haired girl was the prettiest out of the three. From behind them three guys appeared – who were obviously their boyfriends. But Tamara and Blakely did not feel like the odd ones out any longer because those three were also entering Stanton High School as freshmen. Blakely also felt she could have avoided the trio if she had stayed in Bell. But she was with Tamara and that made her decision worth it. Kennedy, Jessica, and the black-haired girl named Angel were besties and their guys were on the football team. Eric, Mason, and Tyler were freshmen and they played football since they were kids. The three of them were closely bonded by sports and cheer. They were athletes, popular as hell, and the three girls made cheer squad. Blakely and Tamara played sports and were never once in cheer.

None of them knew what the six of them were doing there until Eric, Kennedy's boyfriend, announced, "We heard there was a party at the reservoir." He was kinda dumb but had the physique of a Calvin Klein model. Mason was with Jessica, whom they all called Jesse, and Angel was paired with Tyler, who was a bit more reserved, with shaggy, dirty blond hair and pale eyes; he was *beachy*, as though he'd been surfing. They often called him NATO for his last name Spompinato. Tyler and Angel were both petite – it was cute. Blakely felt as though they could be friends, but Kennedy and Jessica were another story.

Kurt and Frankie stepped out of the water.

"Anyone want a fire?" Kurt asked. Kurt was big and bald. He had a genetic disorder and didn't grow hair.

Frankie, being Italian, was dark featured.

Tamara thought of Jessica who called her ugly. She brushed it off then but hoped not to see much of them. But there they were, and Tamara wanted Blakely to sit with her by the fire but wanted the pairs of three to leave them.

Frankie went to his truck. He came back with a cooler filled with beer. They drank the cheap stuff.

Blakely didn't drink beer. Tamara drank with the best of them.

She cracked one open and watched as the others scampered away to sit on a log of a fallen tree.

"Are they friends of yours?" Cherish asked with dark eye liner slightly smeared around the contours of her eyelids.

"Hardly," Tamara sniggered and the rest of them exited the water. Evidently Skye finally said *yes* because they emerged holding hands. Archie looked pleased and Skye was kosher with sitting between his legs. Cherish lit a smoke and Jason rolled a joint. Lacy and Skye were offered a beer. "I don't drink that," Lacy said in a sweet voice.

"I have something for you, momma," David said, and he dished out a six pack of wine coolers from the cooler. He cracked it open for her and she put on her shirt and Blakely felt awkward in her wet underclothes, too. The rest of them dressed away from the fire. Lacy and Skye didn't appear to fear the opinions of Kennedy and her crew.

Call me ugly now, Tamara thought as she slit her eyes at them.

"Didn't they come here to join the party?" Frankie was confused.

"I guess not." Kurt brushed them off.

Cherish took Jason by the hand and they walked the shoreline while staring at the stars.

"They need to talk," Joe said and then laughed, "or they don't want to share their pot."

"Probably a little of both," Frankie laughed.

Joe parked himself beside Blakely – he seemed fixated on her. Like he wanted to get to know her better. David kissed Lacy on the neck. She smacked him. It was puppy love. Tamara broke Joe's concentration.

"Let's find our rides," she said, because they hadn't figured out who was taking them home yet.

"We're all catching a ride to Frankie's place," Joe offered.

Frankie lived in the basement of his mom's home where they were allowed to hang – and the place that would eventually become referred to as simply *The Basement.* The girls told their dads they were spending the night at one another's place. It was easy. Michael and Thomas never questioned it.

"Sounds like fun," Tamara said, and that would be the first night they took off to hang at *The Basement.*

Chapter Five

"What was she doing there?" Blakely was buzzed.

"They heard there was a party at the reservoir." Tamara rolled her eyes.

"They were too good for us?" Cherish questioned.

"Looked that way." Lacy was agitated.

"We should go back there and ask what the hell their problem is," Cherish sniggered.

"Should have thought of that before we left." Skye jabbed her shoulder.

"Ouch." Cherish whimpered cutely.

They laughed and gathered at the sectional sofa Kurt used in the basement. The guys sprawled about the room. They smoked more marijuana or *Mary Jane* as they called it. Frankie's mother was home, but she was in bed by the time they got there. They were sure to be quiet or she'd stop allowing them there. If they were quiet, they were in the clear. Tamara and Blakely passed on the pot. They were dazed among the fog. Tamara's brothers smoked occasionally she knew, but their dad wasn't okay with it. "Would leave you brain dead," he would say, and Tamara joked she didn't need to get any more stupid. But she was bright, and Blakely was, too. They just enjoyed a good party and company; I blamed Mom. It was her

54

genes we were carrying to the parties. She made us who we were. Mom hadn't called since she left the birthday party, but Adam said there was a new hire at the casino – a boisterous and perky woman named Sam. I wondered why Adam cared – he said Sam had a daughter and she knew Blakely, but he couldn't recall her name. The casino was Mom's high life. Her way of life fit our own at the time. At least like Dad, too, we were willing to work. I had the little souvenir shop to tend to two evenings a week and daytime hours usually on a Saturday but there was more money to be made at the casino. Too bad our stepdad owned it, but we were too young anyway. You had to be at least eighteen to tend the tables and twenty-one to tend bar. My souvenir shop was quaint and located downtown next to an art studio. Blakely was the artist – her work was often featured on the school walls in junior high. I thought she could get a job there during her college years to teach art and pottery making. She was good at both.

The crew crashed at *The Basement,* and they awoke in the morning just short of having to report to work. Tamara was behind the grill in the coffee shop and Blakely seated guests in the dining room. They were busy. That was the morning Adam and I sat in the coffee shop to have breakfast. Tamara made us omelets and home fries. She cooked fast and it pleased the busy crowd. When we were finished eating, we went to visit Blakely, but the dining room rush was still head on and her tables were full so we couldn't be seated. She told me she had a ride from work and that she wouldn't need to be picked up. They later hitched a ride with Jason and

Cherish – they wanted to take Blakely and Tamara to the pool and the girls were excited. The pool belonged to Cherish's cousin, Rick, who was attending Stanton with the rest of their crew. Cherish had a nice little VW Cabrio and they let the top down for the ride. Archie had Skye and Lacy in the water when David and Joe showed up. David moved swiftly to Lacy's side and wanted to help her into the pool; he picked her up and threw her high into the air and she managed a massive cannonball. The boys laughed. Blakely laughed with them.

"Jerk," she said, and they took a running leap off the diving board. Tamara wasn't amused.

Tamara touched the water with her toes – the water was warm like bath water. The day was hot, and it was July 3rd, Saturday, so Cherish and her parents threw a party; it was Sandra's sister's house. Jason was good on the grill and Rick, eighteen, didn't cook. The girls were not allowed to drink – Cherish's mother would not be responsible for underage drinking. Sandra was pretty, blonde, and petite, and looked like a model from a cooking show. Blakely wondered how Cherish was so goth-like; her folks were plain and conservative. Jason won them over. He was familiar with formalities from his own parents who owned some of the local real estate businesses. Together they had it all. Cherish brought out the crabs and they ate by the bushel; the entire crew was there: Frankie V, Jason, Kurt, Joe, Archie, and David (who they called Scrat), and who were a group of teenage boys who played Little League together and their girls Cherish, Lacy, Skye and the newbies, Blakely and Tamara, were a group of vivacious heart throbs who had the world at their feet.

Blakely needed the water; she often pulled double shifts on Saturdays and Sundays for the extra money and being on her feet those twelve hours made her legs hurt. She spent much of her time in the water and in the jetted tub. The girls were allowed to have their boyfriends present but they ultimately kept their distance in front of their peers. Sandra made lemonade and Cherish gave her a wink followed by a little sigh; Cherish liked a little rum in her beverages. Her mother would hear none of it. The wine coolers and forties of malt liquor came later during the parties. Cherish just told Sandra she was staying with Lacy and Skye whose mom they told they were staying with Cherish; eventually Tamara and Blakely would do the same and pull an all-nighter; there were nights they all slept in the car. Cherish had her learners permit before the rest. Then it was Lacy and Skye's turn. For the moment they enjoyed the water, crabs, chit-chat, and boys. Except for Tamara who had Blakely and they put their heads back and let the jets take their minds off work; it was Saturday, but tomorrow would be the Fourth of July and in the morning, they had work; at night they had *The Rock* and then they would crash at *The Basement* where they would go all summer.

Rick burst out loud breaking Blakely's reverie when he talked about Florida. Blakely knew I wanted to go to Florida to study marine biology, and Blakely thought about how much she'd enjoy the warmth year-round.

57

"You gotta tell them about senior week," Rick told Cherish, who had just come back from a stay in Florida for the class of '99. Rick was eighteen and wanted to study in Florida; he was spending the rest of the summer at home, then he was to head back to Florida to study business administration while he worked at the hotel as a concierge. Rick was a short and round fellow and was quick-witted; he wanted to study business and then obtain his Masters in architecture. Archie told him about his own family's businesses in carpentry and remodeling houses; Blakely spoke of Mom and Steve and how they owned the casinos and resort.

Blakely wanted to fit in and preferred having something good to say in the moment she felt she could relate. Tamara, too, had a family who was building a home on the farm but that dream was fading away as her father was on the verge of losing the farm; he wasn't making enough income to pay the property tax. Tamara stayed quiet and listened as they chatted about taking off to Florida; Tamara didn't want to lose Blakely and her own future wasn't certain, but she felt she could take up culinary arts just about anywhere. She wanted to be where fate would take them.

"Senior week…" Cherish said and she peered over her shoulder to be certain Sandra wasn't listening… "maybe we need to go there next year," she really felt sneaky. There was a mysterious presence at the thought of going to senior week early; Tamara and Blakely were freshmen, and the girls were sophomores. Hanging out with seniors was the cool thing to do. I was a senior, and

Adam graduated a year before me, the same as Rick – they were in the same class and Adam didn't go for senior week since he knew his dad had prepared the shop in his honor – Adam had the shop to run while his dad was away and got to fix an old Mustang to sell. The sale would pay for his place to stay while taking up studies in mechanical engineering with the intention to work for the prestigious Disney Corporation. We had it all figured out and never imagined anything could wreck a dream.

In two weeks, Blakely would turn fourteen on July 27th but before her birthday it was July 4th and there was an explosion of teenagers at the place they called *The Rock*. Cherish wasn't supposed to drive the little Cabrio without an adult and Sandra forbade it so the girls simply got a ride with Jason – Cherish was lucky he won them over – and together they went toward the reservoir where they found the trail that would lead them to the party – the party was lit and it was only nine p.m. Most of Stanton High School was present and their rivals were Bell High School students because during the high school football games, the greatest known rivals were those two schools.

Cherish, Lacy, and Skye emerged from the vehicle and Blakely and Tamara were on board; they took a seat at a fallen tree and the guys lit a bonfire. The night presented a dark sky, full moon, and a blanket of stars. The girls took off their flops and touched their toes to the water; they wore spaghetti strap tank tops and cut off jeans. The guys showed up in pickup trucks and Kurt and Joe first spotted the girls.

59

"Hey ladies, want to take a ride?" Kurt was the driver.

"A ride where?" Cherish asked, and Archie went over to greet them.

"We're getting some of the green…" Kurt was implying pot.

"We'll just wait here for you to get back." Cherish was frank.

"We're not going to smoke it out here," he was trying to be subtle.

Cherish rolled her eyes. "We'll be right back," she huffed and she climbed into the crew cab of the truck. Kurt was sixteen and was going to be a junior along with Joe, Archie and Frankie. Blakely was in a rush to be fourteen. To be a freshman – to be in high school – but the summer was the best time for everyone. David gave Blakely a wink; she thought about how the guys called him Scrat – he was a little guy. Blakely then turned her face to the boulders across the water on the other side where they would climb *The Rock* face to jump several feet into the water below; she knew she didn't want to be in a bra that night. Tamara kicked back on the log and asked Blakely if she wanted to kick up her feet; Blakely tossed her legs over the side and stretched her legs as if they were playing footsie under water. They were close. Real close. The love they had for each other was paramount. There were more vehicles showing up and there were many unrecognizable faces among them; there were high school teenagers bonding in social circles across the rocky bedding beneath them and they brought music, beer, smokes, and reefer. They were the cool kids. At least they all thought so at the time.

The fires became larger and still inconspicuous; the area was expansive, and they were shielded by a thick and dense deciduous forest that only had one trail leading them to the bonfire parties. The teens had a secret code to get there; *The Rock* was a secret among them and only friends of friends were invited to attend.

Cherish and the gang showed up after thirty minutes; Cherish, Lacy, and Skye appeared from the brush alongside Archie, Joe, David, Kurt, and Frankie. They became a clique. They became bonded through socializing over pot and beer. They had each other and they had a place to go where they felt secluded, safe, and comfortable. Then there was a commotion across the dam where some of them were not from Stanton and Blakely wondered how she could possibly go to Bell where her age wouldn't have them. Bell High School students were not from their clique; they were not welcomed among the social circle. Then Blakely cringed because one of them was Samira…

"She's going to be my stepsister," she told Tamara.

"You mean that's Samira?" Of course, Tamara knew our family story.

"Yes." Blakely wasn't sure what to do.

"You know her?" Cherish was listening.

"Her name is Samira. My Dad's girlfriend's daughter," Blakely just talked of her casually but the other clique from Stanton wasn't having any of it from their biggest rivals. Blakely was only discontent because Samira knew her family – but she was partying there too – so maybe she would be cool, too. Samira was pretty with her dark hair and green eyes. She was unique and accentuated with gold jewelry. Blakely was a bit less feminine in comparison and Tamara was more the tomboy type. The students from Stanton High could be heard yelling from across the way. A group of boys were approaching them, and Blakely's crew decided to investigate. Bell High students were not invited, or at least they thought they didn't belong, and then the shouting turned to shoving and pushing. Blakely didn't think; she just acted, like the day she stood up for Tamara, and she got between them.

The guy being shoved appeared to be with Samira; he was calm, composed, and maintained his cool. Blakely recognized him as Jared Dalton – they went to junior high together but he was a year older. He was from a military family and his mom was Japanese and his father was African American. Samira and Jared looked at one another and then back toward the boys from Stanton and Blakely stood between them.

"I invited them," she said, and the boy backed off for a minute. "She's with me. She's my stepsister."

Jared was a black belt in martial arts and a wrestler; he would be on varsity teams and those teams would be in competition with the Stanton kids.

"Well don't invite them again," one of the boys, Troy Matthews, said.

"They're cool," Blakely said, and she looked to Samira.

"Yeah, whatever." Troy was smug.

Samira pulled Blakely to the side, "You didn't have to do that," she said.

"I know." Blakely was sort of shy and awkward but she still had composure.

"Nah," Jared approached them, "that was cool what you did," and he motioned for a fist bump. Blakely had made the cool list for Bell High. Jared met with a group of friends who were just looking for a place to hang out. He was approached by Billy, Herb, and Alex. They were big guys who bench-pressed and were known throughout Bell, but Blakely did feel as though they did not fit in.

"Man, they almost crashed the party," Archie said as he put an arm around Cherish and they smoked cigs and witnessed the commotion.

"It's all good now." Blakely was keeping it cool.

Jared talked smoothly to them, "Hey," he said,

63

"my friends are cool. I mean we just came to chill." He had no fear.

Samira sighed, "I don't know," she said, "maybe we should just go do our own thing."

Billy, a stout and strong type, shrugged, "Go where?" He was more into watching the party than wanting to leave.

"There's nowhere to go," Herb was adamant.

"There's the pool hall," Alex said. He was a slender guy dressed in jeans and a flannel, cut off at the sleeves, despite the weather.

Blakely had heard that the kids from both high schools had a fight there only weeks before. The pool hall was called *VIP Billiards* and was open until two in the morning. The kids went there since there were no age restrictions – they didn't serve alcohol. The kids kept alcohol in their cars and many of them smoked outside, too, whether cigarettes or marijuana.

Samira was joined by her best friend, Rachel, who was a tall, full-figured, dark-skinned girl who looked like a future model. Rachel liked to be called Simone, by her middle name, and preferred the pool hall over outdoor bonfire parties.

"Let's go," she said to her boyfriend, Billy.

Samira and Simone did not drink, smoke, or do drugs. But they liked to watch the men play pool. "It's like geometry," Billy told her, and she decided to let him teach her how to play; they still preferred to watch but they would play as couples every now and then.

Jared was eyeing one of the other girls at the party who turned out to be Vivian Clancy – one of Kennedy's girls – and another from the cheer squad. Blakely thought Vivian and her friends looked different from what she thought they would look like.

"Who are you staring at?" Samira said to him and broke his gaze.

"I'm just checking out that purple dress over there." He laughed, and Blakely took the comment as being genuine – maybe he was just caught off-guard by the purple sun dress.

Blakely looked around – where there was one, she thought there would be another, but Blakely did not find the Kennedy crew and Vivian had only been with Chrissy Laine as far as she could tell. Kennedy was cheer captain and Vivian was a talented cheerleader herself. They never missed a stunt. Then Samira waved her off and they left for the pool hall where Blakely hoped they would not come close to a fight.

Chapter Six

Chrissy Laine was a strong girl and she intimidated Blakely. Vivian Clancy was equal to Blakely's size and was more robust but shy and beautiful. She was lean but had curves and quite an ass for being a teen. Chrissy and Vivian were waiting for the Kennedy crew to show up – and Blakely knew it. Turned out she was right. One thing with being able to go to Stanton was Kennedy and her crew. It was like Kennedy had Chrissy who acted as her bodyguard; she was always performing the lifts and she spent years training as a gymnast and because of it her body was strong. Blakely played lacrosse and was quick; she had that going for her.

Angel was with Tyler, Jessica (only her friends called her Jesse) was with Mason, and Kennedy had Eric. They were the teeny-bop heartthrobs. At least that's how it's viewed looking back. Blakely and Tamara didn't have boyfriends and they were often glared upon by the other girls who did not understand them. Kennedy walked as though she had a purpose; her friends were equally poised. Eric seemed serious but so did Mason and Tyler. They were the team jocks. Their girls were cheer goddesses – they were a walking cliché. Blakely was average in income until Mom found Steve, and Tamara was the poor farm girl who silently sat in the back of the class until she met Blakely.

Kennedy, Jessica, and Angel gave love hugs to

Vivian and Chrissy and the guys dropped the cooler; they drank beer and belched like men. They had no problem fitting in with the partygoers despite their more ritzy and fabulous background. Chrissy lived in a mansion down by the humane society; her parents owned racehorses and vast acreage. Vivian lived in a fabulous condo with her single mom; her parents divorced a year prior. Rumor was her mom got the big-time money in the divorce; her father was a very well-known surgeon. Vivian was gorgeous to look at; she had long, naturally curly hair, fair skin, and ice blue eyes. She wore baby-doll dresses and sandals. She was precious.

"Gag me with a spoon," Cherish said, whose darker appeal was not without prejudice. Lacy and Skye laughed; like Samira they were bi-racial and had brown skin, but they did not go without prejudice as they looked to Kennedy.

"Rich girls," Lacy said, and Skye sighed, "Well we all can't have money." She rolled her eyes.

Lacy and Skye lived in a middle-class community while Cherish lived modestly as well; her mother was a waitress and her father was in insurance. They had a simple life; all of Blakely's crew had an average income. Archie and his crew mostly liked cars. They lived in houses; they had detached garages. They liked cars and built engines. Blakely enjoyed her friends. She was disinterested in Kennedy mostly, but the Kennedy crew often glared as if with hatred. They wanted to rule the school with their popularity and wealth. Blakely and

Tamara had the gut-wrenching feeling of seeing them daily. In gym class. Alone in the halls. They shrugged it off so they could enjoy the party but there was friction that made Tamara think of the previous year's turmoil – they had a lot of nerve calling her ugly.

Tamara drank a mango flavored wine cooler and thought about her brothers, how they didn't like her being at those parties, but how they wouldn't stop her either. She felt safe. Unafraid. Unlike she had been when Blakely was there that very first day of eighth grade. Blakely and Tamara walked from our house often to the watershed and reservoir where they would take the short trail to the water's edge and dip their toes in while chilling out on a fallen log. They were approached by Jason and Joe – Joe always had a thing for Blakely since the day they met. Jason had been fishing when he saw them hanging out. They chatted briefly and Jason told her about the parties and said they should attend; Blakely was still holding her secret about joining Tamara at Stanton so she simply told them she wanted to go to Stanton but was destined for Bell. Joe shrugged – he didn't get involved in the drama because he was a cool and collected kind of guy. Then Tamara and Blakely met Cherish; the reunion at the reservoir felt fluid, like they were meant to be friends, and Blakely felt part of the in-crowd for the first time. The gang didn't go to the same junior high school, but they were now destined to be in the same high school. Looking back, Mom probably would have signed for her to attend Stanton anyway but due to her lack of parental involvement, Blakely took matters into her own hands, and I supported her.

The one person she was not cool with was Kennedy; she felt a chill run up her spine as though her worst enemy was a predator who would stalk her if she dared to speak her name. Blakely was always quiet, so speaking for Tamara that day was on a whim, but she felt reassured in speaking up for the person who would be by her side as the best of friends. Blakely thought she would show that night, but she did not. Vivian and Chrissy seemed to like Troy Matthews and his crew: Rob, Chris, and Jeremy. They were buddies and of course they played football. Vivian cozied up next to Troy while Chrissy looked over her shoulder, directly at Blakely, and stubbed her nose, flicked her hair. Chrissy was clearly with meat-head Rob. They were talking about Blakely, probably about the little standoff between them and the Bell High students – and there was Blakely, once again, on the opposing side. She thought about going to the pool hall too, but she didn't want Samira thinking she was following her. They stayed at the party instead and the music began – that's when Tamara would perk up and sing along to the latest pop song, but the music would be Alanis and she would not want to sing over the music – she wanted to listen and just enjoy the moment.

Lacy and Skye finally showed up with Archie and David when Kurt, Frankie, and Joe crashed the party – they were loud. They were drunk and Cherish was their designated driver despite Sandra not wanting her to drive. She learned to drive from her cousin Rick who put her behind the wheel of anything with a motor; Rick knew Diesel and Sherry and they often fixed up Rick's cars. Rick would buy them cheap, and Diesel would fix them, and Rick often raced at the local track.

Diesel and Sherry were my best friends. They were a year older than me, Rick and Adam's age, and I was in my senior year at Bell. Diesel and Sherry were at senior week in Florida where they also attended bike week and Diesel came home with his first crotch-rocket. They were bonded by cars. We were all a connected clique in a way. Rick knew Diesel since elementary school, and they grew up in the same neighborhood. Cherish and Rick were cousins but she wouldn't meet Diesel and Sherry until much later since there was an age difference, but Rick taught Cherish how to drive and helped her buy her first car – and later, Cherish would teach Blakely how to drive and Tamara would too, because her own brothers taught her to drive just about everything they had on the farm. Blakely felt like the only person who could not drive aside from Lacy and Skye who had a late birthday in November. They would all drive however in their sophomore year. They began to drive at age fifteen, but first Blakely had to turn fourteen.

And that's when I surprised her. I booked a stay at a quaint little hotel in Florida and I told Blakely we would be going to Florida … and we were taking the Jeep. Adam and I packed the hauler with our gear, and we tossed their bags inside; Tamara and Blakely rode in the back seat and we kept the top down. It was the end of July and in one month we would be going back to high school – me to finish my senior year, Blakely and Tamara to begin as freshmen, and Adam was beginning classes at the local technical school – that is until he and I could move to Florida. It was perfect. The plan was perfect. We intended to room with Sherry and Diesel while we rented a house and pursued our studies; the only downfall was leaving Blakely but she would have her own ride by then and she could move as she wished later.

She and Tamara were loud in the back of the Jeep. They flirted intentionally at cute boys … at least appearing that way, and Adam looked at them in disdain – they were young, but they were having fun. He was modest most of the time, but he let them have at it. Blakely hesitated at first to leave behind the girls, but she looked forward to palm trees and the beach. She needed it. We needed it. The drive was thirteen hours from Virginia where we lived, and it was mostly a straight shot south. We thought about stopping in Georgia at a cool little hostel there, where Adam had stayed with the guys and did some mountain biking. Adam was athletic and adventurous. He did a tandem jump from a perfectly good airplane in Florida a year before we met. Since he turned eighteen, he began training to be a certified skydiver. He also had his master divers permit for deep sea diving. There wasn't much he didn't want to do, and he planned to introduce Blakely to diving. In the winter he could go skiing or snowboarding too, but he loved the heat and the intensity of water. Of the thrill. Adam was a good role model for Blakely and Dad felt that way too – he felt she was safe where Adam would be.

We were traveling at night and pulled over at a truck stop so Adam could catch a few hours of sleep. Adam drove the Jeep only when I needed to catch a

break. He needed the rest stop too, since he was too
unsure of himself to not fall asleep. We slept there in that
truck stop in Georgia for six hours. The hostel was only a
mile away, but we didn't make it there. We went on the
road early at five a.m. and we made it to our hotel three
hours later. Check in was not until four p.m., but they
said they'd let us in at two. We were beat, but we pressed
on. We got out into the sand; there was a place to eat
overlooking the ocean. We went upstairs for the best
view. Later that night there was to be a band and it was
right out the door and a short walk from the hotel. We sat
at a table for four. Blakely ordered the hot cakes and
Tamara had the same but glazed with strawberry. Adam
got the fisherman's plate of all-you-can-eat breakfast
since the place had a buffet.

      We always let the top down. The *Sunshine State*
nurtures the soul. You just feel better there. We walked
out with our stomachs full and our hopes high – and
that's when she saw him. Her jaw dropped and she just
stood there transfixed. He was a golden god of a bronze
color with sleek, long black hair. He was Native
American, she felt dumb for not knowing before, but his
hair was long and this time he had fresh clothes and was
sharp looking – he must be older, she thought. He was
alone and she didn't know what to say but she looked to
Tamara, who didn't notice.

      "I've got to go to the bathroom," Blakely said. The
very day my younger sister turned fourteen, she found
herself lusting after a boy. She went into the dining hall
where she followed him and dipped behind the wall. She

wasn't the most social girl, but she didn't want to let the opportunity pass. She walked toward the restroom marked for women and scuttled inside. She checked herself in the mirror – she was good and sun burnt and had rings around her eyes from her sunglasses. *Perfect,* she thought, *a lobster wearing shades.* Then she made an exit while pondering how she'd never have this opportunity again – and it hit her – right in the chest – all six feet of him.

"Hey," he was startled, "have we met before?"

"We have." She was coy. "You're Chadwick," she said.

He bellowed a laugh.

She felt awkward.

"That's what my buddy calls me," he finally said, "Sedgwick."

"His name is Sedgwick?"

"Yep."

"So … he calls you …"

"That's right. I'm Chad but he calls me Chadwick."

"Cute."

"Thanks." He blushed a bit.

"Where are you going?" She was eager.

"I work here."

She looked let down.

"Oh." She was morose.

He noticed.

"What's wrong?"

"You just must be so much older than me." She tried to play it off.

"I do hear that a lot," he said.

"Hear what?"

"That I look older."

"Oh?" she said.

"I'm seventeen."

The relief swelled in her face… not that much older, she thought.

"I'm only fourteen. Today." She almost didn't add that.

"Wait, today is your birthday?"

"It is."

"Then we should celebrate…"

"Sure…"

"I get off at nine," he said.

She immediately wondered how she would get out but found herself saying, "Sure, I'll just meet you here."

"Awesome …" he paused a moment, "but I can't remember your name … Blake …"

"You're right. Almost. It's Blakely."

"Blakely, that's it," he snapped his fingers.

"My birthday is in a couple months … soon I can pick you up … but how about a walk to the beach tonight?"

"How could you pick me up?"

"In my ride … I already have it. But I'm on provisionals."

"Oh. Cool. Wait, do you live here?"

"Yeah, but hey, I've got to work. I'll see you tonight."

And he took off.

Blakely walked outside.

Tamara was disgruntled, "Where were you?"

"I had too much to eat." She blushed and patted her stomach.

"Eww." Tamara laughed.

Blakely didn't know why she didn't tell Tamara she met Chad – likely from the fact that Tamara hated boys, especially around Blakely – but more because she was too shy and thought she'd only screw it up.

We arrived at the condo where we were staying and washed, changed, and hung around waiting for evening. Blakely was waiting to see Chad again, but we didn't know it. She didn't do anything special or out of the ordinary. She put on faded stonewash jean shorts and a tank. She coated her lashes in mascara and put on her favorite shade of coral lip gloss. We were going out that night to the local seafood joint, but Blakely patted her stomach again.

"I still don't feel too good," she said, and her stomach gurgled. We believed her. She convinced Tamara to enjoy seafood because she had been looking forward to going all day. Tamara loved Alaskan snow crab legs and rarely had them. She told us of the time she went with her cousin Jaime to an all-you-can-eat seafood place before they closed down – that was four summers ago, and she hadn't had them since. Blakely curled up on the couch and brought the cover over her head. She looked like she needed rest. Tamara looked back and Blakely pulled it over her face while the door softly shut. We went to *Dick's Place Seafood Hut*, and I chatted with Adam about going back to our place with a stock of wine coolers and he agreed. He wasn't twenty-one yet and definitely got carded. He sported a pretty kind of look that bar owners never trusted but often he got away with it at the stores; he said it was the tattoos. I'm sure he was right. Tamara ate her crab legs in silence before chatting about taking a plate back to Blakely.

Blakely was love struck. She went ga-ga for a boy. I wished she had told me, but she took matters in her own hands. She climbed out of the comfy sofa and slipped into her sparkling sandals with pedicured toes that were painted a classic red. She dazzled. She walked a block to her destination, where she found him walking across the parking lot. She grinned as he took off his shirt and beneath that tee-shirt was a body of a weightlifter but without the steroids; he was cut and lean at the same time, and his bronze skin glistened in the sun. He let down his long hair; he looked like a rock star. She loved it. She walked briskly toward him thinking entirely the whole way how she'd feel if he whisked her away.

But he started with "Hello."

And she smiled a big toothy grin with straight, pearl-white teeth because five months ago her braces were taken off. And she was thankful for that.

Chapter Seven

"Hey," she said back nonchalantly, "how was work?"

"Oh, you know, work was work," he said as he pulled a cleaner, fresher tee over his silky body.

"That's cool." Blakely had one hand on her hip.

"Where you thinking you'd like to go?"

"I can't be long…"

"Is someone waiting up for you?"

"Just my sister and my best friend."

"Oh, okay, I see…" he said.

"Yeah, I came with them."

Blakely was bad at breaking the icy layer that engulfed her demeanor.

"No problem. We can do something simple like walk the beach … there's an art exhibit."

"I like art." She was trying to stay calm.

He led her to his vehicle, a new, shining four-wheel drive pickup truck. "I just got this from all the money I saved," he looked proud, "been working since I was twelve."

"Where do you work? At the restaurant?"

"No. Definitely not. This is my second job...for the summer."

"Oh, okay, because don't you still go to school?"

"I do. I go to a local public school like the rest of the kids around here."

"No reservation?"

"Nope. Me and my family moved to the beach, and this is where we stayed."

"So what's your other job?"

"I work at a warehouse and make a killing using the forklift and stuff like that. My cousin, Sedgwick, he works in construction so sometimes I help him out, too. He does that mostly on the side though and his main job is using a street grinder or jack hammer ... you know..." and he pantomimed the reverberation of using the machine.

Blakely laughed. "Yeah, I got you. I mean, I know what you mean..."

"Don't look so nervous." He smiled in a charming kind of way, and she brushed him off.

"I'm not nervous," she said.

They walked the beach and came to the art exhibit and other vendors; the streets were blocked and the festival was lit.

"Isn't this supposed to be just art?"

"Nope. It's the local festival, too. Sorry, I forgot to mention that," he said.

Blakely knew we wouldn't be there because we drove in the opposite direction to get to the seafood hut. Tamara didn't want to be without her long so when we got back, and she wasn't there, Tamara was upset. Blakely showed an hour later but not until after she had Buffalo burgers and funnel cake. The local festivity was for honoring indigenous people; it was called the Pride of Native People Festival and Chad fit right in. Blakely tanned a dark shade of brown, but she admired their attire and beautiful eccentricities. The native people were enamored in feathers and played the drums. They ate good food and danced in the streets.

"The whole purpose is to bring awareness about native people."

"It's beautiful."

"What is?"

"Everything. The dance. The clothes. The people here..."

"Hey, there's Sedgwick now ..."

"You dumb fool," he bellowed, "you found a girl."

Sedgwick, who liked to be called Taz because of his tattoos, walked briskly toward them. He was Mr. Cool with a Mona Lisa smile and great dimples. He wore his hair long, too; they honored their elders' firm beliefs in that a great warrior can be perceived through their having long hair. Blakely felt somewhat uncertain among them as if she didn't belong but their spreading awareness of the beauty of indigenous people moved her – as if she wasn't already firmly in love. She really didn't know it. She didn't know what love felt like, but there was chemistry between them; even in their youth they knew that one another thought so and that both moved and compelled them to get to know one another a little deeper. She was able to relate to the indigenous pride of hard work; Dad instilled in her the belief that hard work pays off in the end. She told him of her job at *The Poet's Corner* while Sedgwick reached them when Chad said, "Don't you remember Blakely, from the reservoir? She was just telling me about her job."

"Oh, that's cool. The reservoir? You mean in…"

"In Virginia…" she said.

"Right. Yeah, it's kinda hard to remember."

"I know. I understand." Blakely wasn't surprised.

"So you're from Virginia?" Sedgwick was making small talk.

"Yes. I can walk there …. I mean, we live just up the street from there."

"Cool," he said, and extended his arm that was covered in ink, "my friends call me Taz."

"I see your tattoos." She smiled as he shook her hand.

"I guess Chadwick here might have remembered meeting you at the reservoir." He dutifully punched him in the shoulder.

"I do remember… she was with another girl…

"Wait a minute…"

"Yeah, something is coming back to ya now… go on…"

"You had a friend who didn't seem to like us much."

Blakely couldn't deny it. "She's just a little protective." She downplayed her disdain just a bit.

"Just a little? I thought she was going to throw her left hook…" he stopped, "no, I'm sorry, I'm just playing. She seemed totally cool."

"She's my best friend."

"Is she with you?"

"She is…"

"Maybe you could hook me up."

"I could try." Blakely mustered a smile.

"I'm just kidding." He dangled his keys from his finger and waved them vigorously.

"You trying to get out of here?" Chad was taking the hint.

"Got a date," Taz winked.

"Gotta go, my man…" Chad said, and they high-fived before Taz turned to Blakely, "it's nice to meet you," he said and lightly touched her shoulder.

"You, too," she said softly, because calling him Taz felt off. Like she just met him.

"I still call him Sedgwick, which you might guess is why he calls me Chadwick."

"I'll call him Taz from now on."

"Yeah, that's cool. He prefers that. Oh, and uh, what's your friend's name again?"

"It's Tamara."

Blakely couldn't hang out much longer. He walked her toward the hotel, when she told him she'd have to meet up again sometime. They both looked one another in the eye, "I hope to see you again, sometime."

"Me too…"

"Before you leave maybe?"

"Maybe." She gave him a reassuring smile and he had a hard time walking away.

"I lied about my age by the way."

"What?" She wasn't amused.

"Yeah, I'm fifteen." He laughed. "That's why I walk to work … but, uh, Sedgwick is sixteen and has his license and all that…"

"But your truck…"

"Yeah, but the provisionals…"

"Why didn't you tell me?" she said.

"I'm sorry, I just thought that maybe you were already sixteen."

"No," she said sweetly. "I'm only fourteen."

"That's good." He chuckled, his hand to his chest, "because I just turned fifteen."

She looked toward him, the sun behind him, and put her hands on her hips, "I just turned fourteen today! Remember?"

"I'm glad that's out," he said. He was awkward, a bit too like Blakely, and she learned that day that he would lie initially because he wanted to know her and that they had both assumed one another was older.

84

Blakely walked back to the hotel and stopped on the way to admire some of the paintings done by indigenous women. She was awe-struck and momentarily jealous; their paint featured women of dark skin, hair, and eyes with high cheek bones, full lips slightly parted, who dazzled in turquoise. She stopped at another booth to purchase a necklace and she admired the moccasins on their feet – their native garments and indigenous flair was exciting. She took the turquoise studded bone choker in her fist and smiled at the prospect of knowing someone so beautiful. Chad was fifteen, worked hard, and already had a truck. Then she saw him, quickening his pace to catch up with her.

"I forgot to give you this." He flashed her a seven-digit number. "It's my number." He smiled. The internet hadn't caught on yet within the indigenous community, but they had landline phones. It would be another five years before Blakely would have a cell phone. Such things were not quite yet the norm.

"That's smart," she chimed.

"Oh, I know, dumb moment," he said.

"No, really, it's cool. No worries. Okay," she beamed. "I have to get back."

"I won't keep you – just be sure to use that number." He winked and she flashed him her biggest toothy grin.

She tucked the choker into her satchel and turned

away, wondering when they'd see one another again.

When she returned to the hotel Tamara was livid.

"Where the hell were you?" she fumed, and I couldn't get a word in.

"I decided to walk the beach," Blakely said shyly.

Tamara didn't give in or let up. "If you're able to go to the beach you're able to have dinner!"

Blakely was hesitant so I chimed in.

"We expect a note next time," I said. Thinking back, I wish cell phones were a thing but they weren't an everyday commodity just yet.

I took off for the shower, feeling Tamara would cool down soon enough.

While I was in the shower, Tamara turned a cold shoulder and played aloof while giving her the silent treatment; it was one of those first moments, first indication, that Tamara wasn't cool with Blakely being interested in a boy and she sensed it.

"I will leave a note next time."

Tamara wouldn't even look at her.

"I'm sorry to make you worry," Blakely continued.

Then Tamara slit her eyes and ruffed up her hair.

"That's the least you could do."

Playing sick wasn't Blakely's forte usually but she thought Chad was beautiful. She melted over the thought of his indigenous heritage; she gained an appreciation of Native American folklore and heritage from our father's mother. Our grandmother Helen often talked about our history being rich in Creek descendants.

"Your uncle was full blooded Creek," she would say.

Her sister married a tribesman.

Our great-great-grandfather, Grandpa Earl, was also Creek and he married a woman from Kenya so our grandmother had roots that were lush in culture from her maternal side of the family. Her paternal side was Welsh and Scottish and our grandfather, Grand-daddy Horace, was German; his mother escaped Germany when Hitler was massacring the Jews. His mother had a thick German accent when I saw her last. We were a family of the oppressed society and Grandmother Helen loved to tell stories. They were all deceased by the time I reached high school, except for Grandpa Horace and Grandmother Helen. My father still had them and so did we. They were strong survivors of the Great Depression and taught Dad all he instilled in us about hard work. Dad knew many trades from Grandpa Horace who worked the steel mills, the dredging company, and the unions. They were men who worked with their hands in strong labor jobs. My mother didn't have a similar past; most friends and other folks wondered how my mother and my father could have decided to be together at all but that's because they were only seventeen and their union was strictly superficial; they were both very good looking. You couldn't see the Creek in my father who was bleach blond and blue-eyed since birth because he had traits from his own father; Grandpa Horace, who we called Pap, passed his genes onto Blakely and me since we both had fair skin, but Blakely stole the recessive genes with her thick, long, jet black hair. I had the recessive red hair to coincide with the fair skin. With Tamara alongside us with the dirty blonde hair, I liked to joke that we were like a pack of colorful candy. Adam laughed too because he had all the "beauties in different colors." It seemed that Adam loved Blakely and accepted Tamara like a sister and Tamara did share Blakely with us, then, but she wasn't open to others. Not girls. Not boys.

Tamara came around after she got her word in – Blakely went out and didn't bother to inform us.

"She could have been dead out there," Tamara huffed as I pulled the towel from my wet head.

"She could have," I gave in. "But she wasn't so let's move on." I just wanted the drama to be over.

"Okay…" Tamara hesitated.

"She won't do that again."

Tamara nodded satisfactorily.

I shut the bathroom door and began to blow dry my hair.

Night was approaching, and Blakely wanted to catch the sunset. Back then we were using disposable cameras.

She wanted to capture the osprey nest over the ocean, and we all realized she was feeling better then – and certainly we thought she had been walking the beach just like she said she had been.

Her demeanor was chipper, and she smiled with a kind of glow about her. There were pay phones by the beach, and she said she wanted to call Mom. I didn't expect a thing, so we went out. She captured shots of a purple sky behind an osprey feeding its baby. The setting sun was exquisite, and we didn't want to miss a moment of that beautiful sky while Blakely went to the phone booth to call Mom, but to find out later – she called Chad and Taz answered the phone.

"Hello?" He sounded pretentious following the caller ID.

"Hey… Taz…" she was uncertain.

"I knew it was you. Not too many area codes start with …"

"Yeah, I'm using a pay phone," she said.

"It's cool. You looking for Chad?"

89

"Of course…" She felt happy. Exuberant.

"It should be for me." He liked a bit of swagger.

"I'm sorry… I…"

"Hey, Chad, man…" he was yelling then. "It's that girl." She could hear him in the background.

"Blakely?" Chad was smooth.

"Yeah, it's me," she said.

She looked briefly over her shoulder. Tamara had taken the camera and was taking in the evening sunset. Blakely was typically shy and speaking with Chad seemed to be out-of-the-ordinary for her. She was impressed by his heritage given our father's mother and that part drew her in – like all the years of mystique were intended for her to meet Chad. It was a realm of surrealism in a way. This native boy with rock-star long black hair and a flair of elegance to his demeanor captivated her.

"When do you have to go back?" he asked and she muttered "tomorrow" between her lips as if the world would come to an end.

She told him her address. She gave him her number this time. She hung up the phone thinking she'd never see this boy again, who lived in Florida, and then she wondered what brought him to Virginia in the first place. But she didn't think of that and hadn't asked before hanging up the phone.

"How is Mom?" I asked. Looking back, feeling stupid.

"She found my brown shirt," was her response. I didn't ask any further questions and none of us suspected a thing.

Chapter Eight

We drove home back to Virginia thirteen hours on Interstate 95. The Jeep had a small hauler in tow full of gear. Adam fastened his board to the back and talked anxiously on the ride home about relocating to the beach, about studies, about opening a mechanic shop, about riding waves, and visiting Key West. Senior week would never be enough, but we had that to look forward to until we could get there permanently. Blakely, and I didn't know it then, had a desire for Florida, too, since she found Chad. Had she known the way the rest of the story went, she would have found a way to run straight into his arms before the nightmare of her relationships would ensue.

We arrived home and unpacked in the evening. Tamara returned home and had her brothers' dinner made before she would talk with Blakely again that evening. They talked every evening. Tamara told her what she made for dinner (that night was honey glazed ham, sweet potatoes with cooked onion, and mushroom and asparagus in butter). Blakely didn't cook. Tamara learned early by the age of eleven. She had been baking since ten. Her brothers packed leftovers every night for their next day meal that they would heat in a small microwave they had in a guest house – a one-room shack with minimal lighting and exposed electrical wires. Something that wasn't up-to-code and nevertheless provided ample heating during winter nights when they would be out to bring the horses into the barn. They got up at six a.m. sharp and tended to the farm till night. Because they worked so hard, Tamara cooked and filled Bonnie's shoes. Her father was appreciative. Thomas liked her buttery potatoes the most, but sweet potatoes were in line for his next favorite. Tamara told the restaurant owner, Tony, of *The Poet's Corner* about her vegan meal (sweet potatoes, onion, and mushroom) and they had it added to the menu. When Tamara brought her home cooking to the restaurant, she was already getting a head start in her vocation; Blakely still worked as a hostess and picked up serving tables. On Friday nights they had a buffet and then she worked doubles on Saturdays and Sundays. She would earn two hundred dollars per day and still picked up Tuesday evenings for a co-worker who had troubles with her baby's father. Blakely was enthralled at a young age in an adult world. She was fourteen and mostly served breakfast, as the restaurant was known for its all-day breakfast.

Blakely was determined to leave food services behind and tossed around the idea of becoming a veterinarian, but was fickle about exactly where she saw herself in ten years. A discerning fact between two best friends: one knew precisely where and what she wanted to do, and then there was Blakely who could draw, paint, play lacrosse, and land almost all straight A's, but be totally clueless about how to spend thirty to forty-five years in a vocation. I was destined for Florida to take up marine biology and eventually care for the wildlife at the local shows there. Blakely must have entertained the idea as well when she began talking veterinary science.

It was in anatomy class when she abandoned that idea because dissection was grotesque and cutting open flesh wasn't in her league. Tamara cooked at the restaurant and cooked at home. She spoke passionately about opening her own restaurant. Most of the other girls in school found it odd that Tamara knew anything about vegan cuisine as a poor little farm girl. Tamara was therefore eclectic and multifaceted when it came to food. She happened to be strolling along in a grocery aisle when she picked up *Food Magazine* and fell in love with the richness and depth of vegan food; the colors were vibrant and the assortment of making tasty greens involved utilizing spices that don't pair with meat. She was hooked. She served vegan as a side dish to meats that came fresh from the farm; she felt better knowing that the livestock was well-kept at her farm, and treated right, unlike factory farming was known for doing to animals that belonged on the farm. Tamara instilled in Blakely the idea of how to care for something other than herself, and Blakely felt she could totally get that because we had a cat named Bell.

Blakely didn't care for much meat except when Tamara cooked it, especially her homemade spaghetti with sauce that was to-die-for. Her spaghetti was added to the menu at *The Poet's Corner* and the poor little farm girl gained communal recognition all-the-while Blakely became known as *the hostess with the mostest.* The girls at *The Poet's Corner* were all becoming well-known, especially with the regulars. One regular customer, Charlie, visited the coffee bar every Saturday morning, where Tamara would make breakfast, and every Friday night he'd attend the dining room where he would be seated and served by Blakely.

"You're starting to look like Jesse," Charlie said loudly to Blakely, who was stocking fish filets at the buffet.

Jesse was a waitress there and she often ran the dining room alone. The place would be busy, and she'd handle the workload single handedly at times. To be compared to Jesse was a compliment.

"I miss her," Blakely said, because Jesse had recently quit.

"Oh?" Charlie was surprised. "She's not coming back?"

Hence the reason Blakely was running the dining room alone.

It was Friday night, and the girls were both working. Blakely was serving tables in the dining room while Tamara cooked the food at the coffee shop; the coffee shop was a popular place for truckers, who would stop between Virginia and DC. The dining room was more formal, whereas the coffee shop was smoke-filled and boisterous. There was no smoking allowed in the dining room – those were the days when some public places still offered indoor smoking which would later become banned, even in bars. At *The Poet's Corner*, there was a bar upstairs that was known as *The Pub* to locals, because they crafted their own beer, and *Cheers* to everyone else.

That was the night in July when Blakely would keep his first letter in her pocket and wait for a break between serving tables to read in the ladies' room.

I walked outside to look at the moon that was full and orange. An eclipse? Then I thought of you and wondered if you were looking at the same moon.

Blakely exited the women's room and walked outside. The moon was full, orange, and over the horizon. How did he know she'd be looking at the same full moon?

Hopefully you're outside right about now because my letter will arrive in three days. I know how much you like photography and you'd probably love the fullness and brightness on this night of lunar madness … I can just imagine you in Latin class learning of the goddess who bestows her powers upon us.

Blakely would be taking Latin class too. His letter was almost eerie but more alluring to a teen.

It's the end of July and we'll be heading off to high school (again for me anyway).

Chad would be a sophomore.

I hope your first day as a freshman is profound and impactful in some intellectual way.

She had to fold the note and slip it back into her

pocket. She returned to work wishing she could gaze at the stars. Blakely and Tamara often worked on the same night but in opposite sides with Tamara in the coffee shop and Blakely in the dining room; but both closed at eleven and they were planning a trip to a party after work. Blakely kept thinking about his words when she saw Cherish beside both Lacy and Skye.

"What are you three doing here?" she asked as the dining room began to fill with guests.

"Filling out an application," Cherish dazzled in her red lipstick.

"You want to work here?" Blakely was amused.

"Who doesn't?" Lacy chimed.

"This place rocks." Skye was reassuring.

Blakely thought it would be cool to work with her friends.

"I'll put in a good word for ya."

Tony hired the girls to work as servers in the dining room the next day. It seemed half of Stanton was working there. Some only for the summer, and "the girls," as they were called, stayed through high school and worked one or two weeknights and the weekends.

Blakely finished reading her letter by the light of her lava lamp in her bedroom. Chad was outgoing and told Blakely he would be going to high school with the

Key West kids. He had high academic achievement since his father was a prosperous landowner in Southern Florida. They owned a hostel there after being awarded some grounds from a prosperous rancher who befriended Sam Elliott, his father, also named Standing Bear within the tribe. Blakely was eager to learn more about his family and enjoyed the letter that was three pages long. He even thought to send a photo which featured himself, his father, and Sedgwick. Blakely still found it weird to refer to him as Taz, but she liked the name – and he did seem to be as wild as a Tasmanian devil.

Chad was known as Fighting Crow within his social circle at the reservation and to Blakely it seemed as if he held two separate lives – one on and one off the reservation where he grew up in the Southeast. He was of the Creek tribe in Georgia and was schooled there until he turned thirteen; that was when a wealthy casino owner, Tim Blake, gave some shares to the Natives; Sam Elliott and Tim Blake knew one another from a happenstance when Tim drove an RV unknowingly through the reservation – at the time they were only in their twenties and Chad hadn't been born yet. Sam and Tim became earnest friends and smoked tobacco together and Sam learned that Tim Blake was also a wealthy owner of some tobacco plantations across Alabama. The Natives were given his tobacco as a thank you for offering their land to riding. Their horses were drawn, and the men went on excursions through the fields as they walked, talked, smoked, and didn't have a difference between them but the shade of their skin. But Tim Blake worked hard and found Sam Elliott to be a generous man with his land, so he went and offered him property in Florida and offered an education for Chad. Sam Elliott extended the courtesy and Sedgwick was provided an education beyond the reservations in Georgia.

Chad explained that his family moved across Georgia from Alabama when he was born. Alabama soil wasn't rich and prosperous, he joked, and Blakely wasn't amused – the joke was subtle but reservations are not typically thought of as rich or prosperous.

We're move'n up. Chad joked again and that time she smiled.

She loved Fighting Crow as a Creek Native and Chad as a modern name for a gentleman. She thought the name was perfect, considering that Crows naturally fight over food, as she witnessed once when she threw out a blueberry pie onto the frozen ground outside her door; she watched from inside as a crow ate the pie surrounded by other birds – the only one to fend them off was the fighting crow. She mused momentarily when she took out her pen and began to write:

What brought you to Virginia? She began when she heard a knock on her bedroom door, which turned out to be Tamara, and she quickly put the paper beneath her pillow.

"I was locked out of the house," she explained, and Diesel gave her a ride to the house.

"Diesel was working in the garage?" Blakely was

tired and hoped all she wanted to do was sleep until she remembered the party.

"Yeah," Tamara was frank. "Are we still going to the party? You're not dressed."

Blakely had only gotten out of her work clothes.

"You're not either…"

"I was locked out, duh, I just told you…"

Tamara borrowed clothes from Blakely, who thought she might have a peaceful Sunday the next day to write her letter – if she was not conned into another double.

The souvenir shop closed at ten and I was home by eleven to take Blake and Tam to the party; Frankie V was hosting a party while his folks were out of town, and it was there where Stanton kids crowded into the basement on a rainy night – the last day of July.

Frankie had an eclectic array of music and Blake asked for "LaBamba." She was thrilled! She had just turned fourteen and was in the mix of parties, friends, and fun. Dad never followed up when she went to Tamara's and to his knowledge that's where she was, and Mom was, well, absent (most of the time). Tam was with Cherish as the two of them sang along to the music. They partied hard and were in a mix of kids they'd never met. Frankie, Kurt, Joe, and David chilled in the corner where there was pot. Blakely congregated where there was beer and Lacy alongside Skye gave the evil eye to Jason who showed up late.

"Where you been?" Cherish stopped singing.

"Sorry babe, had to wax the wheels."

He was probably the only guy who would wax a four-wheel drive.

"Whose goin' muddin'?" Frankie said above the music.

Joe turned it down.

"What?" Kurt looked confused. "We're not muddin' tonight…we're partying, man…"

But he was overruled. The rain had stopped. The ground was wet.

"I just waxed my wheels," Jason was livid.

"Time to get that bitch stuck," Joe opened the door.

They went out into the night and the sky was gray, but the moon was still amazing. Blakely thought about Chad. She wondered if his life was equally unruly for such a young age.

When they got behind the wheel of their pick-up trucks, they were loaded in booze and that made them even wilder – but behind Frankie's place was an expanse of hills, trees, and farm his uncle owned so no one would be stopping them and they threw open their tailgates, tossed the coolers to the ground, and lit a bonfire the size of Texas.

And the orange moon shed its omnipresence over them like a phantom in the night.

Chapter Nine

Jason threw his arms around Cherish and Lacy pulled David in close. It was a place for teenage young love. They were among friends and fun. After a long shift at the restaurant, Blakely wanted to unwind and so did Tamara who belted out country like the beautiful blonde bombshell singer from that one show … and the crew thought to themselves … with a voice like that, why not pursue music? But Tamara didn't give herself the credit she deserved and only thought of singing as a way to pass the time. Tamara was into Blakely and with their closeness, others often acted jealous because not all relationships could be that thick or deep. When Kurt changed the vibe from country to rock the girls stopped singing and the boys got rowdy. That's when the *muddin'* began and they took off for the hills to kick up dirt and send mud sputtering behind the tread of four wheels.

Blakely stayed by the fire. She wished she could finish the letter. But she knew, too, that she would have that time soon – she and Tamara didn't live together and Blakely would spend the nights alone in her room before going to sleep and she would fall asleep thinking about the dark-toned native of this country who looked like a rock star and she reminisced of how she spent her actual birthday with the best of company – she had it good. In the Rappahannock country they drank until the beer was empty and the night would wane to dawn, and Blakely would stagger alongside Tamara into Tamara's bed while her father slept, and Shane and Tommy were also just getting home.

The next day was Sunday, and the girls were both at work by seven o'clock. To say they were both hung-over was an understatement. And that's how they would drag themselves into work most weekends because they partied like most teenagers whose parents didn't have the leash tied so tight and many nights after work they found themselves hitched to the tailgate of another's pick-up truck in the parking lot of the church where so many unholy things occurred. But they felt an embrace among the stars and the wind that swept their feet because they were living the best life. They were young and they were free. That kind of free spirit got to me and my crew too, so we knew exactly what kind of fun was being had. We had our own cliques, house parties, nights by *The Rock*, convening over beer in the parking lot and just being together – there was no one to stop us. Even when the police were called, we found ways to be together and that was how we spent the summer of 1999.

That Sunday morning was the first day of August, and Blakely got to pass the word about a surprise party she arranged for Tamara, and Cherish said they could throw a bash at Rick's place where there was a pool and she knew a DJ. Cherish stopped in only to show for her interview. She got the job as hostess/waitress for the coffee shop and Lacy and Skye had been hired to wait tables in the dining room. Blakely was tickled that her friends decided to get a job there. The others there were mostly Stanton kids too: Tommy and John were dishwashers and sophomores. Cherish knew them from around school. The girls earned their titles there – *the hostess with the moistest,* Charlie Few would say, as he visited the dining room on Friday nights and on Sundays stopped in for coffee at the coffee shop. The bar seated mostly truckers and Tamara was the highlight behind the bar because she could crack an egg while flipping pancakes; she never got behind and always had their orders right.

Blakely passed the word about a party on the last Saturday for Tamara's fourteenth birthday on August 30th and they would hold the party at Rick's place. Tamara wondered what everyone was talking about from within *The Poet's Corner* and she felt left out. Blakely told her it was nothing more than gossip about who was taking who to homecoming, for those who already knew, and that they were just left out because it was obvious they didn't have a date – Tamara and Blakely were just entering high school as freshmen and neither had a boyfriend. And as the words left Blakely's mouth, she remembered Chad and his letter and she thought about that orange full moon and during that evening she gazed out her bedroom window at a starry sky. As the moon was waning in its orbit around the earth, she read the letter by the light of the moon.

I am happy that I've met you, was the next sentence in a paragraph that was indented and written in a finely wrought hand. *You seem so open and carefree, which I like, and I hope to get to know you more. I'm not sure how we can do that because of the obvious distance between us … but let's say*

Senior Week … and then we might as well say "I'll see you in a few months."

That's better than never! Am I right? And hey, can I call you sometime? I was glad you'd be the one to call me first … I don't want to come on too strong, but I like you! And maybe I'll be in Virginia again sooner. We were there visiting my Uncle Johnathan Nico, Sedgwick's dad, when we were visiting Virginia. His dad relocated for work when construction turned sour in Florida … at least for him it did… and boat repair work didn't pay the bills either. Enough about me … so I'll turn the mic over to you… Blake … hope you don't mind if I call you by that name, Blakely … because I want to hear about you. What's new?

P.S. Perhaps we need to see Uncle John by Christmas, then I'd see you too … maybe.

Always,

Chadwick

She felt his letter was endearing and I also liked how it read; he was well-versed even if flighty in his thought processes. The most important thing was that he was earnest about liking my sister and I was happy when four years later I'd see that letter.

Then Blakely picked up her favorite rose gold glitter pen and she began to write him a letter and wanted to be sure to answer all his questions.

Hi Chadwick,

Her letter began…

I am happy that I have met you, too. Turning fourteen would never have been so fun! Although my sister did throw a great party. I don't think you're coming on too strong. And my sister calls me Blake, too. I'm used to the name. Maybe I'll see you and Sedgwick soon. What's new? Just the same here … working at a restaurant … we have that in common. I don't think too many fourteen- and fifteen-year-olds work … do they? Well, we do. Sorry for the small talk. I'm glad to have your letter. It was fun to read, too. I will call you sometime. Just tell me when is the best time for you? To get a phone call that is ….

For the night she stopped the letter writing so she could get some sleep. She placed the pen onto the letter and stuck the contents into her bedside table until the day after when she would take it out at her desk, and no one would ask what she was doing; Blakely was a straight A student and she did her homework like a pro. She got her brains from our father.

The following day she called Cherish to work out the plans for Tamara's party – in two weeks we all would be back to school and a blow out party at Rick's was in her deck of cards. Tamara's party was the weekend before the start of school. It would be mid-August, and a pool party was what everyone wanted before they moved on to school sports, more work, and extra-curricular activities. Rick's parents were not home. He was eighteen and able to make it on his own. Cherish simply told

Sandra she would be staying with Lacy and Skye. Blakely told Tamara someone at work got sick and she had to fill in. So when she showed up at Tamara's door in my Jeep, Tamara was already surprised.

"I thought you had to work," Tamara smiled.

"Got someone to cover," Blakely was frank.

They hopped right into the back of my Jeep.

"We're going swimming with Cherish," Blakely informed her, and Tamara went inside to pick out a bikini. When she returned, she had changed outfits, too. A little sun dress over the magenta top. Typically going swimming would imply at the reservoir but when we didn't turn down Arthur Avenue, Tamara couldn't guess what was going on – really, she had no clue. Then we turned into the flashy driveway of the estate blocked by wrought iron gates (what years in construction was able to afford), and Tamara cranked her neck to get a view. Everyone parked in the field since Rick's parents' house was well secluded like Frankie's and from that vantage point there were no vehicles.

"What are we doing here?" Tamara looked confused, "there's no one here."

"Just Cherish," Blakely loved the ploy, "let's go inside to get her."

Blakely turned her head and winked. I gave her a thumb up and I didn't pull away until they entered the front door. There were a hundred bodies in that mansion concealed by the dark. Tamara expected nothing and when she walked in, the place looked deserted. It was impossible to keep one hundred rowdy teenagers quiet for long so as they neared the living room Tamara thought she heard the TV. Instead Cherish and Jason, along with the crew of her now close friends, Lacy and David, Skye and Archie and Frankie, Joe and Kurt, were in full view when they flicked on the light and Cherish stepped forward with confetti; they belted a *surprise* that even startled the DJ. That informed the music crew to announce that it was Tamara's birthday bash over the mic. Tamara looked both perplexed and awkward all at once.

This was when I showed up after picking up Adam whose own ride was without a motor. Diesel and Sherry were at this party. It was the perfect time for me to hang with Sherry with a few spritzers while Adam, Diesel, and Rick worked on the motor. It didn't occur to me then that we were all underage – it was the norm for us rebellious and wild teens. I found Sherry in the bathroom fixing her lip gloss. We were both red heads and our guys liked to call us fiery and hot or the two *feisty* redheads … both of which we liked. It was Adam. And it was Diesel. If they didn't find us cute then we had a problem. We were in the mix of Stanton kids who were getting drunk while some of the others were getting high. They kept the pot concealed until they brought out the beer bongs and pretty much said it didn't matter because we were on private property in the hundred acreage that was hidden beyond the brush.

Tamara had the first seat for the beer bong as she was hurled off her feet and she was placed in the human tripod and the forty ounce of malt liquor was poured down her throat. Tamara was never one to puke. We had these parties before when Mom first met Steve and she kinda abandoned her two kids initially for strong party habits herself. Dad was at work. It was my fault after being left to raise Blake. I took her to the parties. Adam watched over us like a hawk. The guys emerged from the garage to check in on us as Diesel cracked open a National Bohemian beer and Adam clutched the Bud in a firm grip. We moved on to shots of vodka with lemons as a chaser and the music was turned up. The lot of us were interesting as some preferred country music but many liked modern pop. The DJ put on a good blend of favorable dance music from the 80's and 90's and British Popular music was up Cherish's alley. Lacy and Skye liked the modem stuff while Tamara was a country girl raised on the farm. The guys were into anything upbeat, but it must include lyrics. They liked grunge, and they liked rock. Adam would put on classic Iggy Pop or some Clash in the truck to change things up a bit.

The DJ, Magic Mike, offered the mic to Tamara who didn't want to sing, so Cherish took the lead and belted out a classic hit that made everyone smile – the girl could sing that well. Her voice was like a bell. Wedding bells. And Tamara decided to put on a show as the more intoxicated she became she danced sloppily but happily to the music. Kurt was kinda pudgy and his dancing was cute – Joe, who they called Titan for his biceps, and David, known as Scrat (the small guy who could fight) were into Tamara which made Lacy a little jealous David backed off and brought Lacy to the make-shift dance floor by the large in-ground pool that had a waterfall feature.

"I was trying to help Joe out," he confided in her.

"Why?" Lacy was cautious.

"He's got a thing for Tamara."

"Thought he had a thing for Blakely."

"He changed his mind."

Blakely was petite. Tamara was stockier. Joe's build matched Tamara. It made sense.

Tamara was all muscle in her swimsuit. She had the body of a gymnast. Blake was one-hundred-twenty pounds soaking wet. Cherish wore a black suit that accentuated her darker, more sinister appeal. It was a one piece with the texture of velvet. Her red, matte lipstick stayed on despite the water. Blakely wore black too but in a two piece while Tamara had a silky lavender and boobs beyond her years. The crew began to dip in the water. Lacy and David waded in the water, Cherish floated on Jason's back; Skye made an appearance in the pool and drifted beneath the cascade from the waterfall feature with Archie at her side. Frankie, Joe, and Kurt (the single ones) decided to initiate a game of volleyball. The crew typically hung out in couples. I hung out by the pool with Sherry who asked if we would be going back to Florida. The music had stopped, and Blakely perked up to hear. I always took Blake with me wherever I would go. This year though I was seventeen and would be eighteen right after graduation – my final year for senior week.

We never followed the senior rule before, and Blakely probably wouldn't have understood that Adam and I wanted to look for places to rent. To be a bit more serious than years past. I knew that she wouldn't want to live without me but it's only natural for sisters to part ways. It's all part of growing up, of maturing, and leading an independent lifestyle. I didn't think I'd be abandoning her at all. I didn't think any jealousy would arise since Sherry and Diesel wanted to go, too. We talked about how we would rent a place together for senior week and how we would then look for places to rent for the four plus years we'd study at Florida State. Sherry wanted to study by the beach. Enjoy the sun. Just be in Florida and survive. We were used to surviving. Our paychecks were not far from the souvenir shop or the restaurants. They provided enough to suffice. To drink beer. To afford gas and make it out of the house to see friends. Our family unit wasn't very tight – I thought Blakely would understand.

Sherry flipped her red hair and twirled a piece of what would be her bangs if she had them cut and gloated aloud about moving to Florida. The music was up by then and Adam returned from the garage covered in motor oil. He kissed the top of my head.

"She's runnin' great now," he said and his face was flushed.

"You look like you just ran a marathon!" I teased.

"Son-of-a-bitch was heavy," he gasped, referring to the engine.

Blakely returned to the water yielding a cola with some hard rum in it. She got her taste in alcohol from our father, who liked to drink, too. Blakely began sneaking sips around age ten and Dad had never noticed. We were blessed mostly for the life of fun, friends, and finances. We were not dirt poor. We were not on the verge of losing our house unlike Tamara who stayed calm in the knowledge of her dad nearly losing the farm. Her folks were older – in their fifties already and Tamara was only, now, fourteen.

She swam beside Joe who looked cute next to her. His ears were kinda pointy and we liked to joke about him being Keebler. Tamara didn't seem to notice really, or she was nonchalant. The party grew in volume when Samira and her gang showed up, too. We were always nervous to see her – how much she could tell our father. How she could blow our cover despite that she was at the same party – a party Blakely threw for Tamara at a house we never said we'd be at and be caught in the lies and the deceit that we were not just spending the night at a house. We were throwing a bash with kegs of beer, the best DJ from town, and occasionally a live band – as if we were perfectly allowed to do these things. As if we'd never get caught. Then, the fireworks ignited from the tree line, and I noticed Joe was gone along with Frankie and Kurt. And Tamara turned to see the spray of purple

printed against the blanket of a night sky … and
shimmers of gold among the explosions.

Chapter Ten

Samira found Blakely first amid the banging of the fireworks display.

"I couldn't stay away from a sister's birthday party," she said, and Blakely turned as she sat by the edge of the pool with her feet dangling in the water.

"Samira, girl, what are you doing here?" Blake was getting drunk.

"I just told you," Samira laughed.

"Oh, yeah, that's right." Blakely was giddy.

Samira hung out with a small group of friends. That night she was with her boyfriend, Jared, who was a quiet and reserved kind of guy. You kinda just wanted to know what he was thinking. Jared was unique like Cherish but not as a goth kid but kind of like punk rock; he had jet black hair and eye liner. His clothes were torn, and he wore bracelets, like metal, a ring on his right hand, and a chain at his side that connected to his wallet. Jared was his own person and most of the kids at Bell thought Samira just liked his ride; Jared drove a Bentley. He had it made for a young kid in school, but when he was fifteen, his dad died tragically in a fire. Jared was left with his insurance money. His dad was a well-regarded fireman. Jared knew his father wanted him to become "normal" *whatever that is,* he last said to his father, to never see him

115

again; but Jared was an original guy in a very normal world – he was the kid who lost his dad. We assumed Samira enjoyed his sensitivity and authenticity. He secretly told his close friends he got a Bentley to catch the girl of his dreams – then came Samira. Samira turned fifteen, entering her sophomore year, and Jared was sixteen and a junior. Samira's best friend was Simone, the girl who was formerly known as Rachel, but she changed it like she changed her clothes. She went by Simone because it was sexy. She was a diva and had a following of guys who'd do anything for her number, but she rolled solo and liked being the sultry cheerleader for Bell High School. Simone was also entering her sophomore year. Their friends were Herb and Alex: two white boys who were known for playing basketball. Their clique was unique. Blakely liked them and hoped they weren't snobs – they turned out to be nothing of the sort.

Tamara's party was attended by high school kids who were as diverse as the stars. Each one was eccentrically clever and cool. Samira especially dazzled in a flashy golden bikini beneath her black skirt and little tank with spaghetti straps. The pool was the place to be and as the moon waned, Blakely looked to the stars, and she thought about Chad. She thought about picking up pen and paper or if anything, sending him a postcard. She looked to Tamara when she noticed Joe had entered the water. They took a drunken shot at volleyball and when the DJ packed up, Tamara noticed a little local country band show up for the next gig. Tamara was amazed and Blakely told her it was Rick who could make the deal happen since he was friends with the drummer. I sat by

116

the band and waited for them to put together their show. Dixie & Dailey were a couple duet, and Blakely thought that could be Tamara someday. She thought Cherish would be a good one in the spotlight too because only at Rick's place could there be such a mix of teenage subculture and that's Stanton High School – a predominantly Caucasian population of the ones from the farm and the counter culture of rich suburban kids. Then, there were the unusual of punk rock, goth, and culturally diverse who made up twenty-five percent of Stanton. Bell High School was similar but far less country kids – Bell was city and more diverse. Stanton and Bell were rivals especially in sports and general interests.

The night continued and the girls got on their boyfriends' shoulders for a game of *chicken* as the girls tried to pull one another into the water to see who would be the only girl left; so with a beer in one hand and another on their ladies' hip the girls got aggressive. Tamara buddied up with Joe for this interaction and the rest were the usual couples. Blakely found herself comfortable with Alex who charmed his way into her heart with *of course you can trust me if your sister here can,* as he hoisted her onto him whether she liked it or not. But she did. And she did well but Tamara was much stronger than Blakely and got her into the water. They were happy. And the band was beginning to play. The last lady left standing in the end was Simone whose magenta-colored bikini almost came off, but she managed to save face and caught it when it began to slip. The boys there had their hopes up, but the girls were smart and went for the shoulders. The boys needed to exit the water to stagger for their next round of brew from the kegs that housed the local lager. I knew Mom and Steve were friends with the owners of *The Poet's Corner* where the beer came from, but I didn't feel any connection would be made between the kegs and Rick's place. Tony, the owner, was close to Steve and the locals ran tabs there – a constant *I owe you* kind of deal. Mom and Steve were part of the dart league and Steve played pool.

Dixie & Dailey were all set when Adam came back from running to his house to shower and put on fresh clothes. We sat in our own little social circle since Blake and Tam were the stars of the night because Tamara wanted her bestie in the spotlight too – typical of teenagers I thought back about it. Tam loved Blake and she stayed closer to Blakely and seemed to push Joe away – or did she?

When the band was set we moved the table and chairs from the grass and the stage was fully live. We danced. We clapped. We sang. Tamara in her country twang and Cherish in her indie-kind-of pop star voice – they sang like bells falling into one another's shoulders. At the party they got sloshed. I was happy to be there. To be a kind of chaperone for Blakely then, but I wouldn't always be there. They were one another's worlds. And that night waned to the break of dawn. They were passed out on couches. The place was a wreck, and most had already gone when I woke her up to get ready to leave to go to work, feeling entirely hung-over and we couldn't save face. Our bosses knew it. We couldn't hide. We were teens and we were wild and free – schoolgirls who snuck out at night, and that party wouldn't be the last or the first by any means, but when school started Blakely and Tamara were known well throughout the school.

School began at seven-thirty a.m. in August when the days were still well lit and the sun was up till nine. Stanton was an older high school than the newish Bell High School. I dropped Blake off after picking up Tamara well before the first bell would ring. The girls stayed at the front entrance in the open area where the cliques would congregate with whoever was their *in-crowd.* Lacy, Skye, and Cherish found Blakely and Tamara by the doors to the entrance hall. The school was crowded and there was talk of another new school going up; that idea scared us teenagers because no one liked to lose a friend. Cherish was her usual self, decked out with cherry red lip stain and black clothing. She was the Goddess of Noir in school. Tam, the country girl, and Blake the cute little trendy girl, were written out of a story book. They were characters in a play that no one was watching. Or it wouldn't seem so for a while anyway. Lacy and Skye were average in build and simple. Lacy started wearing glasses with thick red rims that accentuated her smooth features. She was cute. Skye was her flashy sister who liked to paint her face in thick mascara, eye liner and a good primer for eye shadow – a metallic blue that sparkled. Skye had recently dyed her hair purple while Cherish sported electric blue highlights mixed with magenta on black tresses that were cut into a short crop cut. Most of the girls had new fresh looks for their first day of, or back, to high school. Tamara didn't change much but had long, wavy, dirty blond curls that were

French braided into two pig tails and Blake wore the cutest shirt with two suspender straps and cropped top with knee-high stockings and black baby-doll shoes. She looked like she was out of a magazine. Tam sported a small CK tee with blue jeans and holes at the knees. The girls were different in appearance but were besties. It was surreal how well they got along and could be totally different. The first bell rang, and the girls headed off to homeroom. None of them had homeroom together. They didn't have many courses together either except Blakely would be taking Algebra II with Cherish; Blake was in an advanced class. To their dismay they did not have lunch together, either.

Blakely was virtually a new girl in school and would have a lunch period with none of her best friends; she would have to potentially step outside her social bubble to make some other friends. When algebra ended, Blake headed off to lunch at noon — lunch period three. Each lunch was only thirty-minute sessions with fifteen minutes of recess where they could have lunch outdoors or stay inside for a forty-five-minute lunch period. Blake scanned the halls for familiar faces. Cherish left algebra after having lunch period one and Lacy, Tam, and Skye had lunch period two together. Blakely would be bypassing the girls as she left for lunch each day. That's when they passed off notes to one another for each to read during classes where the teachers weren't so strict.

Blakely shuddered at the sound of the bell when she left algebra and found no one in the hall she knew. She moved down the stairs that were laid out with three levels and moved into the line to get her lunch when she heard some commotion at the table beside her. There were four older girls, juniors, staring at her. One of them was Chrissy Laine, who Blake did recognize, and the others at the table beside them were in the same grade – Kennedy, Jessica, and Angel, who were fortunate to have the same lunch period together. The junior girls were Chrissy Line's sister Shay and her friends. Chrissy, Kennedy, and the rest of the girls stared at Blake like they could have her for dinner. Blakely wasn't a rich spoiled teen on the cheer squad, and she wasn't high profile like the snootier Chrissy-crew who came from wealth, Chrissy's dad being a famous surgeon, and she stood out for being small, pretty, and out of her element.

She did not have her friends to back her up. It was awkward. She felt the weight of pressure come down on her as if bricks fell from the ceiling. It was ironic what happened next because Chrissy was first to pipe in, "Look at the little snot," she glared at Blakely like a hypocritical bohemian from hell, "she thinks she's cute." Blakely wanted to die when the lower level of the cafeteria broke out in laughter. Each level of the cafeteria was primarily segregated into grade levels and the juniors predominantly stayed to the lower level amid the sophomores, and the freshmen seemed to be sandwiched in the center section with the seniors dominating the top floor that was also open to the main lobby and the front doors; the seniors liked to congregate in the lobby nearing the end of lunch. Blakely was a sheep among the wolves and then it got worse because their boyfriends even joined them at the table; Troy Matthews and his boys were there to make things worse. Mason put his arms around his girl, Jess, then there was Kennedy and Eric and Angel and Tyler, Rob and Chrissy, and Blakey scanned the floor to find, also, Troy and Vivian Clancy – the entire floor was littered with the cheer squad crew and their jocks. Blakely assumed they planned their schedules that way but because she was in advanced courses, she did not have her friends in her corner.

"She's just boney," Kennedy snorted, and the girls and their guys erupted yet again in laughter. The line moved forward, and Blakely entered the mess hall thankful to be out of their sight for just a moment, but she shuddered at the thought of who she would sit beside at lunch – or even what table she would sit at in the freshman station – she didn't have older siblings to cover her – because she chose Stanton, she chose Tamara, over Bell.

Blakely was served her steak and cheese with fries and moved briskly toward the second level when she heard, "Run little piggy," from the mouth of Troy Matthews but to her relief she heard another voice who said, "Blakely," and she turned toward him. "You threw one wicked party!" She was relieved to know only one other person at a table of strangers – it was Joe. Blakely was known around school for hosting the famous party. She had a cool factor the others didn't like.

"What are you doing among the freshman?" she said in a near whisper.

"They host the hottest parties," he joked.

"No, seriously?" She had a seat at the table knowing the rest of the kids at the table were likely to be freshmen.

"It's okay, I know you're serious … so, this is my younger brother." They slapped a high five.

"Oh, I didn't know you had a brother."

"I'm the better looking one," he piped in.

"Mom keeps him on a short leash."

"Shut up." He turned red.

"So that's why you don't see him at the parties."

"It'll be different when I get my own set of wheels." He was modestly driven by optimism.

"Like in two years, punk." Joe shot a fist to his boney shoulder.

"Would you quit?" He was laughing while brushing the new bruise with the swipe of his hand.

"I'm Blakely," she offered.

"Yeah, my brother is bad with introductions."

None of them began to eat except the remaining three boys who hadn't partaken in the conversation.

"Are you all friends?" Blakely asked.

"We don't know him," one of them said.

"Oh, okay." Blakely became awkward.

"Hence why I'm sitting here." Joe started to dig into his cheese steak sub and downed his bite with cola to follow.

"I'm Mike," he finally said.

"Everyone's Mike," Joe played.

"Yeah," the other boy spoke lowly, "I'm also Mike."

They kinda laughed.

"My dad's Michael," Blakely was cool.

"We call him Mikey," Joe was beginning to thoroughly embarrass him.

"No, you don't."

"Yes, we do," Joe retorted, mouth full of steak.

"Hey, man," Mike was casual and collected too, "say it, don't spray it."

"Until now I didn't know anybody at my lunch period." It deeply saddened Blakely. She felt truly alone.

"Weren't you supposed to be at Bell?" Joe was

inquisitive.

"Yeah, but I came here for Tamara … and now we don't have any classes together."

"I guess not if you're a rocket scientist."

"I'm not that smart."

"Yeah, you are."

"Okay, I am." She laughed subtly and took her first bite of a cold steak, minus the cheese, on a semi-stale tasting bun.

Her steak was slathered with ketchup.

The other Mike, followed by his friends, left the table.

Blakely peered at the lobby, filled with seniors, and saw the clock when the bell rang.

"Goes by fast," Joe said.

"That wasn't enough time to finish," Mike said of his double order.

Blakely stood up quickly when she spotted Cherish and Tamara beyond the railing of the top floor.

"See you guys tomorrow…" was a half question.

"I'll be here but I don't know about him," Mike said, and Joe shrugged.

Blakely quickly tossed her cold lunch and proceeded up the stairs when she latched onto Tamara from behind and gave her a squeeze around the neck. Tamara turned to find Blakely and they hugged really giddy over one another. Kennedy came idling by and knocked Blakely on the shoulder. "Watch out," she huffed.

"You ran into me," Blakely wasn't shaken.

"No, I didn't," Kennedy retorted, and spoke faintly beneath her breath to her friend Jessica on the right side, "God I hate skanky girls."

She tossed her hair and slit her eyes.

"Ignore that bitch," Cherish said, and gave Blakely a little embrace.

"Fresh meat," they then heard from behind and found Troy Matthews alongside his best buds Rob, Chris, and Jeremy… when Vivian Clancy smacked the back of his head.

She huffed.

He didn't bat an eye. "I'm only looking at you, babe…" he said and she walked away.

Cherish was already down the hall.

Tamara and Blakely were the small fish in a big pond – the only freshmen at the parties – the only freshmen in the lobby in that moment.

The others waited for the seniors to disperse before they could meander down the halls toward third period. Tamara and Blakely began to walk together to their next class – Blakely was studying Latin, and Tamara had biology. They slipped each other a note to read in class and after blowing a kiss, they parted ways. Blake entered Latin as, once again, the only freshman in a class full of sophomores, and there was Shay seated beside the table where she would be.

Chapter Eleven

Blakely took a seat aside Shay who looked friendly enough wearing no makeup but mascara, with a sweet-and-innocent round face and wavy dirty blond hair. Blakely smiled faintly but was met with a blank stare and what she would personally describe as a sneer — she was not personable, then, and Blake shrugged it off. Freaking sophomores weren't exactly welcoming to the new freshmen. Blakely waited for the teacher to begin, and she removed the note from her jean shorts to read what Tam had to say about her first day – so far.

Tamara had some learning disabilities and Blakely often coached her through school. Blakely was the shoulder she would lean on, and Tamara was always the same to her when Mom left. The letter was written in a kind of scribble like she had a shaky hand, and in cursive – when kids still used cursive. There were some misspellings, but Blakely would never fault her for the dyslexia that plagued her in reading and writing. Her best friend in the whole world described her day and told Blakely how happy she was to have her in Stanton despite not having any classes together. She talked about me and Adam and how we were like family and thanked us all for the ride to school. It was chit-chat and those two girls often liked to refrain from gossip because they were better than that.

When the bell rang, they moved on to fourth

period, and it was Blakely's turn for biology. She saw Mike across the room, whom she recognized for the intergalactic space alien on the back of his shirt.

"Wanna be … wanna be … like Mike," meathead Rob said from behind the table who had to repeat biology – if not the entire grade.

He then threw a crumpled paper ball at his back. It was simple – they liked to pick on the freshmen. They were dumb jocks and the immaturity plagued them.

Blakely took a seat beside Mike.

"Ignore them. They're just dumb."

"Literally." Mike laughed.

And they were dumb. But they were jocks and that was likely why they were not repeating the entire ninth grade. Blakely thought Chrissy Laine must be out of her mind – or solely love struck on looks because he was missing at least a few brain cells, if not more.

The class began at the ring of another bell, but it was the last class, and the last hour, of the day. Then Blake would catch a ride from Adam; he had his truck fixed in addition to a new tailpipe and flashy exhaust, which earned Blakely even more cool points because he was older, already a senior, and Blakely didn't have to ride a bus.

Tamara met Blakely in the lobby. When the front doors opened, the sun shone bright and was radiant against an iridescent sky. Tamara sported her cowgirl boots and cut-offs; the pair looked like the country star met the pop star. They were besties in every way. They hitched a ride with Adam in the back of his truck – added more cool points. He had a lift kit and shock absorbers mixed with high sound speakers and the best of the Moody Blues playing from them. It was so dramatic. He peeled wheels, screeched down the street, and headed toward Tamara's house where the girls would get ready for work. It was like living a double life: teenage high school kid by day and rock stars with jobs at night.

I phoned Tamara's house to give Blake the news – Donna, aka Mom, and Steve were having beers upstairs at *Cheers* (so be cautious). We never did know what Mom would say if she knew all the trouble we were up to; we only knew that she wasn't home. Dad did his best but confiding to him about my first menses was a trip. He talked briefly about the body aging and called it puberty and by that time I was grossed out. Blake had it easier because she had me to confide to but being in fourth grade with a menstrual cycle was brutal. Blake was an early bloomer in every respect. She was taller than average too, so she could always pass for being an older kid.

Adam left Tamara's and headed to my place. I was driving the Jeep to school; as a senior, after being held back early in school, Adam was doing Technical School alongside spending only half a day in high school courses. He was in Bell the first half of the day and Tech the second half, so on his way home he stopped at

Stanton. It worked. The girls put on their work attire: collared shirts tucked into black pants accentuated with an apron. Blakely was working as a server that night as a fill-in for a co-worker whose son had gone missing. Justin was my age and had it bad with drugs; the rumor was that he had been a runaway previously. He went to Bell. He was sixteen and a junior like me. His mother was Katherine Knox who married Billy Williams, the town dealer, when they were only kids themselves. He didn't have a chance in hell, they all said. We felt bad for her because she was so dedicated and reliable at work.

I worked the souvenir shop most evenings during the week. Cherish, in addition to Lacy and Skye, had a job at *The Poet's Corner*. Positions at the Golf Resort were seasonal, and the place was full of kids from Stanton. Kids who worked anyway especially at the Resort where most kids spent the summer working the pool, putting greens, restaurant, and fitness center. Kids whose parents might be less than adequate like Donna and Steve; Steve had a kid too once but stopped talking to him until last week when he showed up at the house unexpectedly. Mom said he was loaded – high on beer and smokes. The situation was rough for Mom – although she lived to drink, she wasn't into drugs. Narcotics were mostly for the young and stupid, in her opinion, and so Steve's son, Steve Ewing, Jr., fit the ballad. We merely thought, like father, like son. So maybe we were too hard on him.

That night Cherish and Blakely had an evening of waiting tables. At fourteen and fifteen they could serve tables but were not permitted to serve alcohol until the

131

age of sixteen. Blake never felt so young, even childish. Lacy and Skye were scheduled on the weekend. They would hostess and serve tables as well. They were the *Poet's* crew as they were called by the locals and the regulars chatted about the *"Poet Girls"* who were all so beautiful even if a little on the darker side, like Cherish, who almost always dressed in black.

Tamara was cooking in the coffee shop. They typically worked the same nights to catch a ride more easily. Cherish was due to complete her learners' requirements and get her license. She just needed to pass the written and driving test. Lacy and Skye had November birthdays but would be getting their learners before Blakely and Tamara could sit behind the wheel. The guys were washing dishes and bussing the tables. It was a busy night for both the coffee shop and the dining room. Blakely said the bar upstairs was packed and she hadn't crossed paths with Mom yet. That night would be the first evening they left work together and would meet the crew at the pool hall where Joe, David, Frankie, and Kurt would be hanging out. Archie was due to pick up Cherish who wasn't allowed the car that night – her ride also belonged to Sandra. She hoped the job at *Poet's* would earn her own set of wheels. She wanted a Bug or a nice little Cabrio – the top down going ninety mph on the freeway appealed to her. Her permit was going to expire so she needed to pass her test. She was smart, though, and none of us doubted her.

Archie showed at closing, and the girls were glad to get past the front door without running into Mom, who

132

could be totally sloshed by then. We wondered if Steve
would carry her home. Mom was only thirty-nine then.
She was out to celebrate for the entire week of her
birthday. We were scheduled to see her that Saturday for
a party at her and Steve's place — a two-bedroom condo
with a pool in the common area on the roof. Steve had
another place too, a large garage, and a gazebo for parties
by the lake. She was in her own state of wealth. Blake and
I were expected to carry our own. We never asked them
for a dime, although they had it. Mom was into herself.
But she did on occasion splurge when she took Blake out
for some back-to-school shopping in honor of her first
day in high school. Then Mom really wouldn't be seen
until Christmas, aside from her birthday.

When Archie left with the three girls in tow, he
had Joe in the passenger seat who asked Blakely what he
thought of his younger brother Mike.

"He's great," Blakely responded, and Tamara
looked curious.

"Who?" She could hardly hear over the radio
playing Green Day.

"Mike," she said in her ear, "Joe's younger
brother."

"Oh," Tamara said flatly.

"You don't need to tell her; she already knows."

Now it was time for Blakely to be perplexed.

"How do you know…"

"Mike's mom gets hay bales from his mom," Tamara smiled.

"Weird. Small world." Blake was kinda gullible.

"We are half-brothers," Joe chimed in. "Same dad."

Things started to make sense.

The drive was twenty minutes to the neighboring county where Archie, Kurt, Frankie, and David went to school together. They were all in their sophomore year and Frankie was next to get his license. He had a truck he already purchased and was going to get the tags once he passed his exam. They all had trucks. They all went off-roading and they all stashed beer. That evening, they had a tailgate party in the parking lot of the pool hall where no one was allowed alcohol, but they were in agreement that what went on outside was their own business. They took turns playing pool and then traded positions outside to chat, hang, and chill. Adam worried about her with boys, but I told him Tamara had her back. Kurt was happy as a lark because he scored new rims for his diesel. He boasted about finding them at some garage sale he went to. The crew gave him the courtesy of listening.

"That's great, man," Frankie said, and he almost had his own ride once the truck passed emissions and he could get tags. Frankie worked part-time at the local pizza joint. He spoke about taking everyone to the place, since he was a manager with a key, and they could enter through the back – *pizza on me*, he said in his Italian accent. Lacy and David went outside to meet up with Skye and Archie, and then Cherish and Jason came behind them. They were finished with rounds of pool. None of them felt loaded; they drank modestly. Blakely wasn't a huge fan of beer so she nursed it.

They loaded up in their pick-up trucks and went to *Pizza-A-More* and outside, as they were filing inside through the back door, a police cruiser idled on by. They didn't feel they had been caught and locked the door behind them. They settled on milk crates and waited for Frankie and Kurt to make the pizzas. It was a perfectly warm night in August and the indoors provided a nice, cool atmosphere where they could hang out together as good friends. When the pizzas were fresh, they brought them to the back room where they congregated over cold brews and hot pie. Although it was summer, school was in and most of them had curfew at some point into the night.

Kurt, Joe, and Frankie talked about being single while the couples sat together and conversed in private little conversations. As the night ended, the girls got rides home and Blake entered the door around eleven o'clock but Dad didn't notice. Alisa was sick and was already in bed. That weekend would be Samira's weekend with her dad. Her dad was cool and Michael, Dad, liked him enough. At least they all got along.

Blakely retired to her bedroom and sat by her

bedside at the little white desk our Pap made for her. Pap, our dad's dad, was a carpenter and he made most anything that could be whittled from wood. Pap was alive. Grandma Helen was sent to hospice and was reluctant to recover from pneumonia. Pap, Michael Senior, was almost ninety and had retired from wood working after he made Blakely her desk, and he sold his little shop. It was decided that Pap would come to live with us soon, and Alisa was fine with that. We had a guest room in a five-bedroom farmhouse. We didn't have a farm, but we had acreage – another reason Mom left. A luxurious condo was more her style. Dad wanted to have a boy, a Michael III, but Blakely and I would be all they had. Now Dad had Samira, too, and Samira had siblings from her father, but was Alisa's only child. We were all mostly from divorced families.

Blakely sat at Pap's finely made desk, furbished from mahogany, and wrote Chad a letter. It began with ruminating about her first day of high school. High school was already second nature to Chad who was fifteen, and a sophomore. Blake and Tam were a year behind their entire crew of friends. Looking back, I would have found her more freshmen to be friends with but all she would be left with were Kennedy's crew. But in the heat of the moment, she wrote passionately about being at the Pow-Wow in his company, and doted on how much she loved her herringbone necklace. Later he would send her his grandmother's turquoise stone fastened into a beautiful ring made of twisted metal and fastened into the shape of an infinity symbol. It was such a modern idea implemented into a very precious commodity. He would eventually send that ring as a promise when things get too overkill to enjoy.

Before the turquoise ring, Blakely would receive letters and postcards and they would talk about their favorite things to eat, where they have spent vacations, and places they dream of vacationing. Those letters, phone calls, and postcards were her lifeline to the dual life she had been living. He sent her photos, and she would do the same. They stayed in contact across the miles that separated them with the only means of staying connected that was possible in their day.

Blakely sprayed her letters with her favorite perfume, sealed it with a lipstick kiss, and put it into the mailbox with the hope that another letter would arrive – and it did – the very next day. It was to the point where a letter came daily, and I told Blake I didn't know how he had enough money for stamps.

"He has a job at the restaurant," she reminded me.

Chad's family was much like our own, apart from being an indigenous culture: they too had work, bills, and houses to upkeep. They were modern but had strong roots in the Creek tribe. Florida was peaceful where they were in Key West, and Chad's father lived and worked in Florida designing boats, which began for the Creek first by designing simple canoes, and that skill and passion progressed to designing fishing boats and onto other, larger projects. The Creek prided themselves in bartering still, outside of earning hard cash, so the fishermen provided fish, but also trinkets they collected from the sea – many shells the women would use to make jewelry and clothing that they would sell at the Heritage Days Festivals. Blake talked about Pap and how he could build from wood too – it was nice to have some way to connect to the richness of deeply-rooted culture as a modern American girl. Chad invited Blakely to another festival that would be happening in the fall – a Creek Pride Festival but she wasn't certain how she could go unless she could travel for a four-day weekend during Labor Day. So, she laid down her ink pen and went to sleep while dreaming of music, dance, and the beat of the drums mirroring the rhythms of her own heart.

The next day in school, she continued to think about how she could make it down to Florida. She had both her letters in her pocket. One to Chad, and the other she wrote for Tamara. She told Tam about how much fun she had together, in the back of the pizza joint, eating pizza, chatting over beverages, and slamming the cue ball into the wall during a bad break. They often reiterated what they did together as if the other had not been there. Her letter to Chad went into the drop box in front of the main office where all her letters would go. She wasn't entirely sure why she never told anyone about Chad except she felt the allure of keeping him a secret and she liked the emotional elevation from it. There wasn't much else that could feel that uplifting; receiving his letters made her giddy inside, and like all well-kept secrets she felt it deserved careful attention.

Chapter Twelve

The morning of school began with the girls mingling in the lobby. Tamara and Blakely were kind of like precious sisters to the girls they stayed closest to, like Cherish. Lacy and Skye adored them too despite the grade difference among them, especially since Tamara could sing a few high notes, and Blakely was the beautiful, somewhat shy, and very intelligent cool girl in school. On that morning, Blakely learned that Tamara switched classes so she and Cherish could have music class together; they planned on singing in the upcoming play. Tamara had to add performing arts to her schedule so that she could sing in the musical *Another Time*, a three-act play written by a student who had won a contest. It was scheduled to be performed at the school. Both Tam and Cherish were auditioning as helping acts. Tamara had a dream of making it big one day – a dream that she kept secret from everyone, even Blakely. Tamara wanted to perform on Broadway and wanted to own a studio apartment in New York City. Around most of her friends she kept the small-town farm girl appeal and didn't ta0lk of Broadway to anyone because she didn't want anyone to squash her dreams – even Blakely. It seemed then that Tamara thought about how she could eventually leave everyone, and anyone, to make it big. Why else would she keep a secret?

Tamara put both arms around Blakely and squeezed her about the waist as Blakely stood on the tip

139

of her toes.

"My woman," Tamara said, and they mocked a kiss to each cheek when a voice came from behind.

"Am I interrupting something?"

They heard a laugh.

"Just friends being friends," Cherish chimed.

The girls let go of their embrace and laughed heartily as if they were just caught doing something flirty. But they themselves didn't see it that way, and Cherish totally got them, while Lacy and Skye were uncertain and gave one another an inquisitive look.

"Best friends can love each other," Cherish was defending them.

"Oh, I get it," Joe was adamant, "I was just joshing you." Blakely shot Tamara a look, "What's Joshing?"

"A joke with a cool factor," Cherish was once again the remediation guru.

"Yeah, exactly," Joe was still *joshing* them.

Lacy and Skye felt it was their moment to pipe in, "Who asked you to homecoming?" Lacy was looking fierce with stars in her eyes. She thought Joe liked Blakely and Tamara, and they knew there were bets on which one he'd ask to homecoming. The girls thought a junior would never ask a freshman to the dance, but bets were still on. Then Michael approached them and gave a fist bump to Blakely like they had been cool for years.

"How's it going?" he said to Blakely.

Lacy sniggered because she then sensed the debate was further extended now that Joe had a brother who also liked Blakely, and they made more sense being the same age and same grade.

"What's everyone talking about?" Michael was chill.

"Homecoming." Lacy looked to her sister.

"Have you asked anyone, Joe?" Skye was queuing in on the debate.

The girls' boyfriends knew who Joe wanted to ask but they kept that bit to themselves as *bros* they called it. The girls started to see that he had a thing for both, probably for various reasons, as if one could take traits from both and make the ultimate woman – he did dote on both of them. But Joe was unique as Blakely found out; he was also advanced for his age. He was fifteen and a junior. Blakely had that in common with Joe – they were stellar performers in the intellectual department. Blakely still turned her thoughts to Chad whose ripped stomach, tan lines, and biceps – not to mention the long hair – reminded her of an indigenous rock star that she doted on. She never felt an attraction as rich before; he reminded her of the singer whose long black hair flowed off his shoulders in the music video back in the 90's – just a few years before. She loved the singer and kept his image imprinted in her psyche, and then she had Chad who was like the real-life entertainer.

Tamara broke her concentration, "What are you daydreaming about?" Tamara said it in her deep voice; although Tam could sing like a bell, her natural voice was a bit nasally.

"I want to go see a rock concert," she smiled.

"Like Anthony Kiedis or something?" Joe was point on.

"What?" Blakely was taken aback.

"I told him." Tamara punched him in the shoulder.

"Wait, you told him what?"

"That you have a thing for guys in rock bands, especially one particular lead singer…"

"Right?" Blake was just kinda amazed by his timing.

"Hey, look, I turn sixteen next week…" Joe was hinting at taking one of them to the dance.

"It's okay, I already have a ride," Blakely chimed in as if reading his mind, too.

"Oh, well that's a little pretentious   "

He seemed put off.

"To school I mean." She was dashing the discomfort.

"Yeah, um…" he just didn't know how to proceed.

"What were you going to say?" Lacy was typically pushier than the others, a total contradiction to her sweeter and shyer twin Skye, and Joe began to look comfortable again.

"I was going to offer you two a ride … to school … but now… I don't know."

Lacy punched him in the other shoulder, "No, you weren't."

"Yes, I was." He was meek.

Then the bell rang.

They parted ways through the awkwardness of the moment.

It seemed to Lacy, as she told Skye, he was up to asking Blakely to the homecoming dance but she obviously shot him down – making him very uncomfortable in the moment.

"I don't blame him." Lacy said to her sister in

home economics class.

Blakely was in geometry class and noticed Angel seated next to her own boyfriend, Tyler, who was a class act and had everybody laughing.

"Hey NATO!" Mason called from the hallway with Jessica who was rushing into class. Geometry was full of lower-level sophomores and Blakely felt awkward, once again, in a class without friends. Or other freshmen.

Angie had a sweet demeanor but was in with the snob squad: Kennedy and her besties Jessica, Vivian, and Chrissy – who was also a gymnast, and wasn't at the parties much. But in Stanton High School she was a strong Cheer Queen and a tough competitor in sports. She was popular and all of them were a walking cliché whose meathead boyfriends were accepted into and would be playing varsity football and were only sophomores. They were good at playing football – but they were also low-level geometry students who just needed to pass the class.

That's where Blakely came in. At the end of class, Mrs. Keelor asked if she would consider tutoring some of the JV students. For the first time in Blakely's life, she felt stupid.

"I'm not sure," is all she could say.

She was saved by the bell and took off to lunch.

Before entering the lunch line, Blakely met with

Tamara in between classes and gave her the note as Tam rushed off before the bell to make her way to English class. Tamara liked writing and found herself enjoying creative writing as she also excelled in art and music. Tamara was musically gifted and artistically talented, which made up for her shortcomings in the other courses – home economics was her best subject as she obviously loved to cook. That's where they asked Tamara to tutor, and Blakely could barely fry an egg.

In line for food, Blakely was met with the snob brigade who was seated at the lunch table together as couples – brooding over what they would wear to homecoming. Blakely was certain they laughed at the little freshman who wouldn't score a date. As she opened Tamara's letter, Blake heard Mikey over all the voices in the cafeteria.

"Blakely!" he said exuberantly.

"Hey," she was polite. "Where's your brother?"

"Oh, he changed some courses and has lunch at first period now."

Joe had lunch with Tamara, and Blakely had the company of his younger brother who wouldn't turn fifteen until the beginning of the following year like her. He helped her not to feel so young and out-of-place, but the snob squad cooed.

"Boy toy," Kennedy sneered, and the girls erupted in laughter.

145

"Ignore them," Blakely stayed calm.

"Oh, I will," Mikey was nice.

"Is it okay if I call you Mikey?"

"I don't see why not. All my friends do."

"It's just that my dad is Mike."

"No problem."

As they made their way through the cafeteria, they left the bottom level of sophomores and entered level two where the faces of familiar freshmen comforted them.

"I wonder if the other Mike will sit here today." He looked around.

"Probably not."

"Why do you say that?"

"They were kinda weird."

"Well, they were nerds."

"I guess," she mused.

"Have you thought about homecoming?" She thought she would be conversational.

"No. You?"

"No." She began to eat the pizza on her plate. "I
146

haven't."

"It's totally okay to go without a date."

"I think I will."

"I think I will, too."

"Some of the guys were joking though…"

"About what?"

"Joe likes you."

"That's a joke?"

"Not about you or anything … Joe's just kinda…"

"Awkward?"

"Yeah."

"Totally."

They briefly sat in silence.

"I think he likes Tamara," she was trying to pry.

"He says you're both hot."

"Thanks?" She was candid.

"It's a compliment," he said.

"It is?"

"It is from a guy's … you know…"

147

"Perspective. Yeah, I get it."

They finished lunch together at the table only the two of them occupied, and when the bell rang, they both took off to third period, where Blakely would have Latin with Shay.

But in class it appeared Shay was not there as her desk sat empty. Blakely wondered if Shay would be back to class – or did her presence scare her away?

Then she heard a voice say, "Sorry I'm late Mr. Matthews" and she handed him a tardy note before going to her seat. Shay smelled good and her nails looked freshly painted. She sat down at her desk and removed her notebook – Blakely noticed Shay does it too – she began a note addressed to Chrissy who Blake would see in biology as her last course for the day.

At the end of class, Shay spoke to her for the first time. "So," she began to fold the letter into a tiny square, "could you give this letter to Chris for me?" Obviously referring to Chrissy as Chris.

"Sure." Blakely took the letter and left her desk. She had five minutes to make it to biology where she found Michael already seated.

"Hey, Mikey," she said and handed him the note.

"What's this?" He opened the letter.

"Oh, God," Blakely laughed. "That's for Chrissy Laine," she whispered.

148

"Why did you hand it to me?"

"So I wouldn't have to." She laughed.

"It's got your name in it," he whispered.

The biology teacher asked for one person at each table to come to the front of class to pick up their microscopes. Their lesson was on cell biology and reproduction. Blakely grabbed the microscope when she heard the voice of Chrissy Laine speak to her, "Uh, I believe you have something of mine." She sneered as she spoke, and Rob chided beside her.

"Give her the letter, punk!" He was overly zealous because Mikey turned and threw the letter and tossed it right into the trash to the back of the room – a perfect score. Rob was floored and looked as though he wanted to grab him by the back of the neck.

"Why did you do that?" Blakely whispered.

"It's nothing." Mikey was morose.

"Tell me what it said." She didn't want to let it go.

"I said it's nothing." He pulled the microscope toward him. Organisms moved within the slide in an apparent phase of reproduction. At least that's what he thought he was to look for considering they both barely paid attention to directions. Blakely jotted directions within her notebook for them to discuss later. She felt the hairs stand on the back of her neck as Chrissy and Rob talked furiously to one another about how Rob would like

149

to break his neck for not handing Chrissy the note. Chrissy was a tough girl and Blakely was not a fan of being on her bad side. She glared at Mikey, who would not look up from the scope, and she felt her face go flush.

"Tell me." She tried to be quiet.

"Yeah, tell the wench." Chrissy mocked aloud.

"Excuse me. What's going on over there?" The teacher was adamant.

"They threw something of mine into the trash over there." Chrissy was dead faced and very forward.

"Then go pick it up." The teacher retorted and went back to the lesson.

Chrissy left her seat and picked up a fist full of balled-up paper and returned to her seat.

"Don't read that in here." Their teacher seemed to know exactly what conspired between them.

"What did she do to you?" Mikey wasn't joking.

"Does someone in here need to go to the office?" The teacher cut them off.

"No, ma'am." Blakely was serene.

Mrs. Mansfield stood up and approached them when the fire alarm sounded – and Blakely felt saved by a fire drill, or she thought it was a drill anyway.

They filed outside in the football field where Rob met up with Troy Matthews and their close buddy Jeremy Moon. Chris Kelley soon accompanied them, and their girlfriends gathered in a clique that Blakely found fascinating – the popular crowd was now crowding around a note that said something about Blakely, and Mikey wouldn't tell her what the contents were. They sat in the grass and Blake cringed. She wanted to know. She felt bitter and resentful toward him but she knew he didn't want to hurt her feelings.

Chapter Thirteen

Blakely arrived home and slammed her bedroom door. I could tell that something had been bothering her when she entered the kitchen. Adam shrugged and whisked me away before I had the chance to talk to her. Blakely wanted to be alone it seemed, so I thought I'd find out later. Adam planned an anniversary dinner, so we had a special date; we had been dating since we met at the carnival where he was working the ride and gave me his favorite t-shirt. That carnival was the last one I had been to, so Adam wanted to take us out to the restaurant where we had our first date rather than back to the carnival.

She pulled out the letter Tamara gave her that morning and finally gave it a read. In the letter Tamara spoke of homecoming. She said she had been asked by a guy to attend but she turned him down. Blakely immediately figured it was Joe – no surprise there. Blake was unaffected and at the time she wasn't mildly curious why Tam would turn him down. She also figured they both would attend without a date – that wasn't a big deal to Blakely. She took out her pen and paper and began a note she would return to Tam the next morning where she didn't feel she had to ask so she simply wrote: *I turned him down, too… so do you want to go shopping for a dress?* She knew they would go together, and she didn't feel so alone – Joe, Frankie, Kurt, and some of their other friends were single, too – it was normal to be single.

Blake then folded the letter and took out her paper tablet and tore another page from the seams and began her letter to Chad – her mind then left homecoming and returned to Labor Day weekend that was around the corner only a week away. When I returned home, she was able to tell me the news; the fire alarm hadn't been a drill but was caused by some of the kids who lit firecrackers off in the boys' bathroom. All this would have been easier if there had been the advent of social media, but we were nineties kids. Blake was able to talk about the dead heads who thought lighting firecrackers in place of smoking pot in the boys' room would be an adventure; it was outside where she had her own little adventure, but not in a good way. The snob brigade came out full force to taunt Blakely; ever since she stuck up for Tam against Kennedy, she had her pick of the litter. Blake became the little runt in the pecking order. Her average size and lush curves made her appear older, but Blake was a softie. She wasn't a fighter – and looking back neither was Kennedy – she just carried a shrewd demeanor, but Blake was no fool either; she could carry her weight in academia.

Blake still hadn't talked to me about Chad, but she mentioned Labor Day weekend and asked if we'd like to take a trip to Florida. I didn't really see it in our cards. I told her I didn't think we could go so soon. She appeared morose and I couldn't fathom why except Florida was beautiful and I assumed she wanted to be at the beach.

"How about Ocean City for a weekend?" I

interjected.

"I've never been there," was her response, and she blatantly walked away. I didn't know what I did to piss her off. I wanted to grab her by the shirt but instead I decided to listen.

"What did the Kennedy crew do to you?" I asked politely.

"They called me a skank and acted like they could vomit – are you happy now?"

I wasn't.

"Is going to Stanton worth all this?" I asked her patiently.

"Yes. I want to be with Tamara." She looked sullen and I flat out felt bad for her. No kids should be that cruel. It seemed to me there had to be a better reason to ostracize Blakely from the cool club. In fact, other than Cherish, Lacy, Skye, and of course Tamara, Blakely didn't have a club – the cheer team, like the debate team, and so on, had their clique and the school was just segregated based on interests, intelligence, and economic status. Blakely and her entourage of friends were eclectic and that was unusual. Stanton was full of clichés like the meatheads, the dead heads, and the snobs — it was full of haters and those who beckoned love, peace, and happiness, except from anyone who wasn't in their social circle.

I strongly felt Blakely needed to go to Bell but I didn't want to be pushy, and I wanted to support her. I just wish my sister confided in me, but she was always so reserved and private. Although I'm not sure how she felt comfortable opening up to Chad except she was love struck; she loved that indigenous flair and pride of the Creek. It was empowering to her to bask in his positive energy, especially since she was on the receiving end of negativity at the high school.

Blakely breezed through her subjects; she just caught on easily to information. I wasn't quite as excelled and brilliant as Blakely, but I was her big sis and I wished she knew I'd always have her back. I left her bedroom and she stayed for a while in her own solitude, which she did often. Lacrosse season was coming in the fall, and she would become busy with academics, sports, and work. She really wouldn't have the time to keep up with her big sister and I also was busy with the same load as she. Other than dropping her off at school in the morning and Adam picking her up from school, we wouldn't see one another a whole lot. She learned a great deal of responsibility early on. That's why I thought more about her trip to Florida and wanted to mention the prospect to Adam, but he was working on cars that evening at Rick's place. I phoned Diesel and then Sherry to find out their plans for the holiday weekend. I thought that I could get them on board with another get-away before we were immersed in the ins-and-outs of high school requirements. I tried Diesel first. I wanted him to talk Sherry into it if possible. It turned out it had to be the other way around; we, the girls, needed to convince the

155

guys … until that following week something very cool happened: Adam won a trip to Florida from a sweepstakes he entered on the previous trip – the trip included an offer for a free tandem jump. Adam was ecstatic, to say the least – it turned out that we didn't have to try convincing the guys very long.

"Who will he take sky diving?" Sherry thought she was being tricky. I knew she wanted to go; Sherry was athletic, cool, and a major adrenaline junky. She wanted to go badly. I told her Adam wanted her there (and he was totally cool with it) and he would have to continue trying to convince me to sky dive. I wasn't the risk taker that Sherry was: She grew up with her father, who took her rock climbing, hiking, kayaking, and mountain biking. She was made for stunts that only daredevils would do. When I told her she was going, she phoned Diesel to tell him they were going back to Florida. He didn't have a choice and his love for her was thick; he would do it for her.

"I wanted the Chevy back on the road before Christmas," he retorted.

"It will be, baby," she said and laughed.

He loved his rides as much as she loved a good rush.

I didn't tell Blakely right away. I assumed she would want Tam to go along, too. I had to figure out transportation if Diesel's rides were in for repair. Sherry was working on getting her own ride and for sure she wanted a Jeep. The tough girl in her wanted a motor that could withstand off-roading. I had the image of her getting stuck and Diesel fishing her out – she would be that kind of chick. No amount of mud would stop her from getting her boots dirty. She just had saved up around seven thousand to put a down payment on the Jeep; she worked the golf resort and the very wealthy golf pros tipped her well. I tried to get a job there, but they never had an opening. Then Mom and Steve owned the golf resort, and I didn't want to work for Mom. I was a tough case, but I did my own thing. Blakely was the same way. We couldn't work for Mom no matter how much money it would make us. It was Mom's absence that made us cringe at the prospect because we became adept at raising ourselves.

On a Tuesday night, Blakely had work and I planned to stop in and give her the good news. "Adam won a trip to Florida!" I jolted her out of her seat. She was rolling silverware and cleaning tables.

"What? How?" She wasn't fazed.

"A sweepstakes kind of thing."

"Is it legit?"

"Yes!" I was dying for her to be excited. "We can leave right before Labor Day – maybe even take off Friday."

"I have to find coverage." She was skeptical.

"We'll find coverage and you can go." I smacked the table for effect and with that I walked away leaving her to figure out how to find someone to cover her shifts.

It turned out easy. She found Cherish, who was willing to work. Cherish also said she spent her last day working the concession stand at the golf resort; Sherry had the job there long before Cherish and we were all just beginning to become acquainted. Sherry worked as a caddy and porter for the golfers. The concession stands closed at the end of the season. As a seasonal position, Sherry had to get another job beginning in the fall; likewise, the souvenir shop would close house for the winter months. Sherry and I applied to work in retail.

"Oh, okay, now I know who Cherish is," Sherry said when she arrived at the restaurant. I rang her at home to find out if she got her new ride… and low and behold she did! She passed her driving test and was ready to go with her own set of wheels. She was to meet me at the restaurant, and we would let the girls wait on us. Then Mom and Steve walked in right in the middle of our dinner to tell us that Sam, their new receptionist, needed a fill in over the weekend – and they wanted one of the girls to be there. The resort stayed open through the winter and guests stayed to take advantage of the beautiful and exquisite snow-capped mountains. The restaurant there wouldn't close but experienced lay-offs for the dwindling tourism – the girls never could get in at the restaurant there. The Poet's Corner was the next best thing to The Pub (aka Cheers), and kept people coming into the restaurant; guests would eat in the dining room before going upstairs. It was seasonal there, too, in a sense, because the Stanton kids would work there while school was in session.

"Sorry, Mrs. D," Cherish said apologetically, and called her Mrs. D since they bought out the resort, "we'll be here at the restaurant."

"All of you?" Mom gasped.

We didn't want to tell her about the Florida trip; we didn't need her trying to be Mom when it made her look good, especially to her friends. There was a time when Mom wouldn't let me go on a camping trip with Adam because her best bud Cindy wouldn't have agreed with her lack of parental dictatorship.

"I need someone on the phones," she retorted.

"Why can't Sam do it?" Blakely was annoyed. She just stayed an hour past her shift to serve me and my friends, and then she had to be in Mom's scope of awareness.

We wanted to talk Florida. Mom wanted us to work. It was that simple, and it was always what Mom needed or wanted versus what we wanted.

"Sorry Mrs. D," Cherish was finishing waiting on her last table. It was nearing ten o'clock and the dining room would be closing. Steve and Mom were going upstairs to the bar.

"How about you, Blakely?" Steve turned with a
159

toothy grin.

"No, thank you." She was at least sincere.

"I was hoping one of you might be able to help us out."

"Maybe one of you could do it." I winked for effect.

"Oh, Vanessa," Mom was flabbergasted; "we own it. We don't work there." She was really a bitch at times. That was Mom. That was Donna, but we didn't often call her by name to her face. She winced and turned away to head to the bar. Steve had her on the dart league. He seemed too chummy even for Mom, but we were certain she liked his money.

At the close of the dining room, we went to the coffee shop where Tam was still working and Cherish let it out of the bag.

"We were talking about Florida," she said aloud from behind the counter where we were seated, and Tamara turned to face us.

"Who's going to Florida and when?" She was tired from a long shift.

"We intend to go for a long weekend." I smiled and she didn't look persuaded.

"When?" She was drained. We could tell.

"We are going for Labor Day weekend," Blakely spoke softly. She too had a long shift.

"I can't go," Tamara replied.

"Oh. Why not?" Blakely asked, and she wasn't faking her concern.

"I have to work." There was a vacancy in her eyes. Something was amiss.

"I'm going to head out," I said as Adam and Diesel showed up.

Sherry was ready to go as well. We had upper class things to do like paintballing in Diesel's back yard while the others blared country tunes and Diesel would entertain them with a chill kind of rock like some Steve Miller Band. I thought the cherry on the cake would be Cherish's punk rock and maybe Kurt's death metal to add to the mix. But Blakely had her own friends and I had mine, so we didn't always mingle, or hardly at all, except for the pending Labor Day weekend. We left Blake and Tam, who had to finish cleaning house before they could leave the restaurant. That happened around eleven o'clock and Kurt was outside waiting on them. That night, they had plans to hang out at The Basement where Frankie, Joe, Archie, David, and Jason were waiting. They were quite the little group of friends. Outsiders wondered why Tam didn't date Kurt and Blake didn't date Joe, but they didn't, and they hung out as friends because that was enough to them.

Once they were inside Blakely was able to talk with Tamara in private. They cozied up on the sofa and didn't feel good enough for a drink.

"Is something going on?" Blakely didn't know how to proceed really without hurting her feelings or making the tension worse.

"My dad is about to lose the farm."

"I'm so sorry."

"Don't be. It's not your fault. It's just that I need to work to help."

"I totally understand."

Blakely truly did understand. She was someone who could relate to another person, especially Tamara, on a deep and intimate level.

She put her arms around her then noticed they were being stared at by everyone else.

"What are you two doing over there?" Kurt was giddy.

"Get a room." Joe was always cracking jokes.

Frankie and Jason just shrugged and continued talking among themselves. Lacy and Skye decided to lounge on the bed and gaze at the strobe lights Frankie had in his room for affect. They let their minds wonder, and in a few hours it would be daylight by the time they all crashed, and the next day was Sunday.

Chapter Fourteen

Blakely helped Tamara on the farm. She was assigned the task to feed the lambs, goats, pigs, chickens, and cattle. Blakely loved animals, but it was her first time with livestock. It was funny to Blakely that Tamara preferred vegetarian food until she said, "get to know your food and you might feel differently." She could totally get it and she wasn't a big meat eater, either. She particularly never liked steak. She was the pickiest eater out of the family. Tam wanted to explore cooking options and liked plant-based food instead of eating the pigs she was there to raise since they were born. They worked in the farmyard through most of the morning and turned in around late afternoon to make lunch for Shane and Tommy.

"How's your mom doing?" Blakely asked at the table.

It was a touchy subject.

"She's with him," Shane said with a mouth full of sweet potato.

The him still didn't have a name in their household. Ronald Dalton was an imposter, but Thomas had more important matters to tend to after the infidelity of his wife. Without her income, his farm was sinking. He needed help monetarily and the boys were working fourteen-to-eighteen-hour days in place of employees.

Blakely cared for them; she was practically one of the family. Even if she wouldn't exactly be homeless beside them, they still respected her.

Tamara filled in for her mother's absence. She was a strong and independent young lady of that household. Bonnie was seemingly as selfish as Donna had become. Steve and Ronald couldn't possibly see what their presence had done to a family. Dad had at least moved on with Alisa and we gained a stepsister. It would be better if Thomas could find his way to move past the emotional burden of his wife leaving her family for another man. He needed to forgive and stop blaming himself for her adultery; he worked long, hard hours, and wasn't home much. She found a man who could tend to her needs. These matters were difficult for the girls to comprehend.

"Family should always come first," Thomas said as he sat down at the table. He didn't believe in being present at the dinner table filthy, so he showered before he joined them. He had been bailing hay and the workload left the boys sweltering in the August heat. It was the last day of the month and Blakely was thinking about Florida. She felt guilt in the pit of her stomach because the family was suffering loss over a man. She thought Chad could never cause such pain. She wasn't married and committed the way Bonnie and Donna had been — her interest in a boy was innocent, she told herself.

She went home to plan her weekend getaway. She only had four days of school, and then she planned to be on a flight to Florida. A three-hour plane ride was easy she thought. She went to school Monday morning and felt the time drag on as she went to lunch and stood in the line waiting to be served tacos or chili dogs. She avoided the Kennedy clan by a minute; she had her food and was making her way to the table where she would find Mike, who already had his tray of tacos.

"Tacos or chili … it's so hard to decide." He was sarcastic.

"I went with the tacos." She sat down and started to put the sour cream on her taco.

"So, I saw that Vivian Clancy and Troy Matthews will be joining us in biology class." He must have known the school cliques as well.

"Will they be sharing the table with Chrissy and Rob?" Blakely rolled her eyes and darted her glare to the table below; they all had each other: Kennedy and Jason, Troy and Vivian, Chrissy and Rob, and Jessica and Mason. At the adjacent table Jeremy, Chris, Angel and Tyler, and Shay were seated – what are the odds they shared the same lunch period together? Blakely could only wonder then assumed they kinda got their way as student athletes who hold up the image for the school. The Stanton community and faculty were all proud; they enjoyed their winnings and gloated at the pep rallies. Stanton football held the title for the longest running season in a winning streak and that title had yet to be broken by any other high school in the state.

"How do you know they're in biology class?"

166

Blakely was trying to be casual.

"I overheard in the main office." Mike was nearly finished his second taco as he inhaled his lunch.

"Does that mean the rest will be there before the end of the season?" She sniggered and Mike just shrugged.

"Yeah, and evidently Shay and Chris are a hot commodity."

"Really?"

"Definitely." They were enjoying the gossip and small talk. "Chris asked Shay to homecoming."

"Not surprised."

"They were kinda a secret over the summer."

"Why a secret?"

"So they didn't step on anyone's toes."

"Whose toes?"

"Jeremy, I guess. He wanted to take Shay on a date, but Chris was already interested…."

"How do you know all the scuttlebutt?"

"Ah, interesting word choice. But, um, Joe and all his friends talk a lot around me."

167

"Do you think Joe likes Tamara?" Blake asked.

"Joe likes you … but I'm not supposed to say that."

"Why?"

"He just thinks … you know, he likes how you look I guess," he said.

"Are you going to homecoming?"

"No."

"Darn."

"Why?"

"I thought we could go…"

"Now who's stepping on whose toes?"

"I mean we could go solo. Single."

"Ah. Right. Okay."

"Does that mean you want to go?"

"I'll have to think about it."

"Wait, when is homecoming again?"

"It's next Friday after Labor Day."

"Oh, cool."

"Why? What's up?" he asked.

"I'm going to Florida for Labor Day."

"What's in Florida?"

"What's not in Florida?" she said.

"Yeah. I mean, I guess."

"The sun. The beach. Palm trees."

Blakely avoided any mention of Chad. She wanted her sacred omen kept safe and she wouldn't tell a soul.

"That does sound kinda nice." He laughed and in that moment the bell rang, and they left for third period biology.

Vivian, alongside her boyfriend Troy, walked into class and took a seat behind Blakely and Mike. Chrissy and Rob had now been assigned to their table; during labs they would work in a group of four.

"Can we switch lab partners?" Vivian was snooty.

"No," Mrs. Mansfield wasn't amused.

Vivian yawned for effect.

That day in class they studied in their groups of four over the microscope to gain an understanding of the diversity in the structure of cells.

169

Chrissy and Rob didn't speak to them. They only spoke to each other, and Chrissy passed off a note to Vivian. Blakely thought she and Tamara were the only nerds who exchanged notes in school. She sniggered to herself thinking they were followers.

Third period ended and Blakely found Adam waiting outside and she went home to her bags that were already packed – only three more days to Florida and she got the mail early to find a postcard from Chad. He had been in Oklahoma at the reservation of his extended family where he and his family made tomahawk steak, made from bison, which they took to Florida to prepare for a ceremony. For the tribe, the coming of the cold season would ordinarily mean the tribe would hunt and store food, but because Chad's family relocated to Florida to earn a living in a modern world, they held a ceremony in thanks for their food, and their abundance. Chad's father was "modernized" in the way of living in an industrial city but cultivated in his passion for his ancestors and taught Chad how to be civil in the way of cultural beliefs and practices. Chad loved telling Blakely of these things and he adored her enthusiasm for his people.

Blakely turned on the lamp by her bedside and she began a note to tell Chad she would be coming to Florida, and she hoped to spend time with him there. She wanted to call him, but it got too late and he would be working. Chad worked most evenings at a restaurant like Blakely did. They often wrote their notes during school hours if they could sneak it past the teachers. Biology wasn't a class where Blakely could do that. Latin was another subject, another story, the teacher there just didn't seem to mind if the students seemed like they were on another planet mentally; she just went on with the lesson and wasn't fazed if anyone wasn't fully attentive – Blakely got A's and so that may have justified her tendency to veer off. She wrote about the pending weekend, knowing it was kinda last minute and she hoped she could see him even if it was just during lunch. The restaurant where he worked was called GL's Shack House which was convenient to the beach and garnered tons of tourists. It was still a hot season for travel in Florida, and Chad would be needed for work. She wondered how he could fit her in, so she looked at the menu he mailed along with a postcard – it seemed as though he had a premonition that she would need it sometime. Chad was like a mysterious warrior to Blakely. He seemed to do the right things, including enticing her to visit by sending a menu full of delectable food items. She found the fisherman's platter to be a nice alternative to steak or chicken, but she wanted something more vegan and found eggplant parmigiana to be favorable. She was excited. She wanted the beach, the sun, the sand, and the boy who could serve her awesome cuisine. She licked the sticky side of the envelope and sealed her letter within. She was ready for tomorrow.

When the dawn broke over the horizon, she went to school and deposited her letter in the outbox in the main office. She noticed the secretary watching her.

"Do you have yourself a pen pal there? Blakely,

171

isn't it?" She said with a southern accent.

"Something like that, Mrs. Dempsey." Blakely was chipper.

"Don't let me bother you." She laughed heartily.

Blakely was in the office and used the outgoing mailbox weekly.

"Oh, you're not bothering me." Blakely waved and Mrs. Dempsey told her to enjoy the rest of the day.

At lunch she chatted with Mike over food and beer because Mike was Joe's brother, and Joe liked her sloshed, as he called it. Mike, however, was more chill and preferred to stay reclusive, while Joe wanted to be the life of the party. Blakely didn't get past Kennedy that day without hearing her daunting voice echo down the hall, "Skank to the right," she hollered, but Blakely kept walking.

She had just come from art where she painted a beautiful oil on canvas of some tulips she had a photo of as muse. The artwork was displayed in a glass case along the hallway of the cafeteria. The art prompted Kennedy and her crew to react cynically as she passed by them. She made her way to the second floor and felt their glare on her back, and it made her hair rise on her neck. Blakely wasn't a fighter and couldn't imagine being taunted into one.

"What's her problem?" Mike sensed her

172

discomfort as Kennedy roared that the awkward Blakely could make her barf.

I wondered later why she wouldn't change schools and go to Bell where she would have me and Samira, but Tamara was that important to her.

"She just doesn't like me." Blakely couldn't figure it out either.

"It's because you're beautiful but not a total bitch." He sipped from a soda bottle and shook his head. "I could throw this at her head." He really meant it.

"No, let's just ignore her." Blakely wasn't as awkward as she was passive. She just didn't let their juvenile behavior get to her. She wanted to eat lunch and get through biology.

It was there that Mike had enough.

"Why don't you just shut the hell up!" he sneered as meathead Rob sat behind Blakely acting as if he was throwing up lunch.

The teacher, Mrs. Mansfield , wasn't amused.

"Who is using that language in my class?" she said hastily as her back was turned to the students while she jotted notes onto the chalkboard.

"That would be Mike," Rob retorted and darted his finger.

"Why did you say that?" Blakely whispered.

"Mike, you need to go to the office now," she said.

"He was acting as though he could barf," Mike was unfazed.

The class erupted into laughter.

"It wasn't a good lunch today, Mrs. Mansfield," he said innocently.

Mike didn't say anymore. He stood up and left the room, leaving Blakely to deal with Rob and Chrissy and Vivian and Troy. It was a couple's nightmare all the time for Blakely. She even tolerated Latin class, where Shay acted innocent and coy toward her but everything she said got passed along to Chrissy and from Chrissy to Kennedy.

"Why don't they like me?" Chrissy mocked in a squeamish tone.

It was an honest question, but no one was interested in giving her an honest answer because they didn't have one – they were snobs. They were wealthy. They were the meatheads and the athletes – they were the walking cliché of bullying and Blakely was a shy, timid, and reserved young freshman who had straight A's and had only one friend in the entire school – a poor farm girl whom she loved more than a sister. Their affection for one another was insurmountable and that's what she felt.

At the sound of the bell, she went to the office to find Mike, who was just leaving then, and he held up a note.

"Detention" he said. "Tomorrow. At lunch."

A hole ran deep in the pit of her stomach – what would she do at a lunch table alone? She never thought she could want detention so badly.

Chapter Fifteen

Blakely tied her apron onto her waist and was relieved to see the girls. Cherish and Skye were there to wait tables and Lacy was hostess for the evening. It was Tuesday night and a very busy evening for the entire restaurant: upstairs was pool tournament night, in the dining room was a ten dollar all-you-can-eat buffet, and at the coffee shop was never ending pasta, which brought in a ton of guests. The place was busy, and Tamara hardly had a minute to see Blakely, as she was piled with orders and Blakely was seated with a full house; the girls were running the show.

Then the Samira crew walked in. She was accompanied by her boyfriend, Jared, and his friends Herb and Alex, and her bestie Simone, who had her arm around Billy Williams.

"I came to hang with my future sis," Samira said, and followed suit with a hug and a light pat on her back.

Jared and Samira held hands at the table.

Simone and Billy had their arms around one another and sat close. Herb and Alex sat with one another.

Billy's dark complexion was sleek like cocoa butter and was perfect like Simone, who looked as though she was wearing smoothing oil. They were beautiful couples. It was that night when Blakely learned that Herb and Alex were a romantically involved couple.

Billy and Herb grew up together. Herb's mother knew about his pending sexual preferences since he was eight and she informed her reluctant husband that they would support him always. All her husband could say was okay. The crew also suspected Tommy and John had a thing, but they were quiet – Herb and Alex were not. Herb had jet black hair and a soft voice and Alex had sleek blond hair, pale eyes, perfect set of teeth, and small stature. They were from equally diverse backgrounds, as Herb was the son of an anesthesiologist and a stay-at-home mom, and Alex was the son of a hard-working single mom. Herb had it all in a neighborhood of wealthy kids and Alex grew up in the rural district of Richmond. Billy met Herb at a central park where they both played football. They had that love in common. Herb didn't grow into football, but Billy was a popular player for the Bell Wild Cats. Football season was approaching, and Blakely felt at odds about going since, Kennedy and her entire entourage would be there. Blake didn't want to be afraid, but they intimidated her. They had each other and Blake couldn't see it then that she, too, had a nice group of friends. Still, she felt singled-out and alone.

Samira ordered the half price buffet that only included the salad portion while the rest signed up for the entire buffet; Simone loved shrimp and there was fresh fish and clams on the menu. Herb and Alex ordered oysters in addition to the buffet.

"You're here to eat," Cherish's voice chimed.

"Hungry as hell," Billy said with a plate of fisherman's platter (on Tuesday nights the fisherman's platter was on the buffet). It was a huge deal, and the place was busy. Blakely had no time to eat. Skye and Lacy mostly bussed the tables while Cherish and Blakely served. Skye was shy about serving and was there to wait tables, but she helped her sister keep up. At the end of the night, the girls split their tips with Lacy and Skye who kept the tables cleared and topped off drinks. They were a good working team.

"You all going to VIP's tonight?" Samira said.

"We had plans to go to Kurt's apartment," Blakely said.

They were planning a round of playing cards and quarters. Kurt turned eighteen and got his apartment with his own money. He worked hard at a car lot, first as a valet and second earning commission for the number of sales he pulled through in a marketing gig and pulled twelve-hour days. Frankie had also turned seventeen the week before, but he had a free place in his mom's basement. Kurt wanted a roommate, but he was the oldest and his crew just hadn't turned eighteen yet. But Lacy told Skye that Archie and David might be renting the apartment.

"How many bedrooms does it have?" Skye seemed bewildered.

"Don't you know what your man is up to?" Samira giggled.

Simone peeled her shrimp.

"I haven't talked to him since this morning, and he didn't mention anything."

"He's planning to rent one of the rooms," Lacy told her. "I just got off the phone with Archie."

They planned on letting them in on that information that evening.

They hustled to clean up the restaurant and bus the tables and roll their silverware. It was eleven o'clock when they got there.

They crammed in Cherish's ride to make their way to Kurt's new apartment. It was a nice three-bedroom place. They now had another place to hang. They played a round of asshole, a popular card game, and they dropped quarters until someone, that being Frankie, wanted to play strip poker.

When Kurt returned from a liquor run, Frankie was naked in the kitchen. His eyes were big as saucers.

"What the hell is Frank doing naked in the kitchen?"

"Strip poker," a fully dressed David said.

They were all tickled to see Frankie lose, since it

179

was his idea in the first place. David finally let Lacy in on the scoop.

"My mom totally kicked me out," he said.

"Aren't you a little young for that?" She wasn't amused.

David's mom was a "Donna" but the street kind. She dealt with drugs, and rumor had it there was a time when she got busted in a meth lab. David being kicked out into the streets was a blessing, or at least better than he fared within the home. David was also seventeen and a junior, and his friends were surprised to see him stay in school considering his home life, but he was wicked smart. His intelligence tests were off the charts. He never knew his father and his mother raised him alone. He suspected that he was of good genes if he could ever find his father. His mother gave him a name and a location. It was like pins and needles for David to consider. His mother only told him his father left while David was an infant. David suspected his father might have been smart to leave her. Lacy doted on David's sincerity and intelligence. Lacy's and Skye's father was a strict and conservative black male who wore his suits and played his cards well. He knew David wasn't what he came from; he had a high-level IQ and was very respectful. Big Keith he was called by his son's friends (Lacy and Skye had an older brother named Tyron) and they respected the man. David knew he had to earn his trust to be with his daughter. Their mother, a bi-racial woman of white and black race, was a beautiful and sophisticated woman

180

who worked for the state after she earned her degree in sociology. David wanted to aspire to their level of maturation, but he never could fully leave his mother. He was good to her and often bailed her out of trouble. It was a difficult position for him to be in.

He told Big Keith he planned to go to college and would be studying business and criminal justice. He planned for the FBI. Big Keith worked in law enforcement prior to the Department of Juvenile Services, which is how he met their mother. Blakely enjoyed their story and retold it when Dad would ask where she was going. She told him about David and how they had an apartment. Dad looked sincere and concerned, "Will your sister be with you?" he would say.

"I'll be with her," I'd say, and Dad would feel a little calmer.

He felt David was like Adam in that respect.

It was okay for Blakely to hang out with older teens in my presence. It's true, I was rarely present, but I also felt Blake and Tam were in good hands. Kurt, David, and Archie had jobs. They were smart.

Archie worked as a counter and parts person at the bike shop. He got Jason a job there with him since he landed a management position. It was crazy that teens could become management, but that's how it worked. Our crew was all working kids from middle class families and that's how we were different from the Kennedy squad. They were the girls who lived in large, lavish houses and had money. Their fathers were bankers, doctors, lawyers, and business owners.

Sherri and I got jobs in retail at a place called Peebles at the time. It was normal for friends to get friends jobs. We all had one another's back. Because Blakely worked Dad didn't feel she was faring too ill. He understood an honest day's work. He applauded her helping Tamara at the farm. He inquired how her father was doing because one man understood another man's good graces. Tamara didn't talk about it much. She survived in school and thrived at work. She loved to cook. The Poet's Corner took her mind off the stress caused by being at home.

"Do you know why Tony calls it The Poet's Corner?" She broke the silence of Frankie being naked. He didn't even put clothes on. He sat down, stark naked, rather than lose his cool over losing.

"No," Jason spoke up. He had grown out a small goatee. "I kinda wondered though…" he was cut off.

"It's kind of, I don't know," Frankie looked for the right words.

"Too girly coming from Tony," Archie said.

"You met the man?" David asked.

"Yeah. The same night you did you nitwit."

"Yeah. Right. I remember."

David didn't seem to remember Archie being there at all but they both met the big boss man after picking up the girls from work.

"Tony, you know, he's a total stud." David looked to Lacy.

Then Tamara spoke up. "His wife is a writer."

"Is she a poet?" David interjected. They were being manly.

"Yes. She is." Tamara was frank.

"His wife came up with the name for the restaurant." Blakely knew the story.

Tony's wife was a beauty and a sophisticated woman. She taught creative writing at the local community college and Tony managed the business. It saddened Blakely's heart to hear of his infidelity with another woman, a waitress in the coffee shop. Her name was Erica, and she was a student at the same college where his wife, Jewel, worked. She really was a gem in Blakely's eyes. But it seemed they saw little of each other since Tony had to oversee the restaurant and his mistress was promoted as manager of the coffee shop. They spent a lot of time together upstairs in the office looking over server checks. He was also cheap, and whatever the servers forgot to charge, Tony would deduct from their paychecks.

Tamara liked Tony and his wife's story because

she too wanted to operate a restaurant. She felt like she fit in there with the rest of the staff. She took to Kurt's bedroom where she crashed, and Blakely fell asleep on the sofa. It was usual for the girls to crash at friend's houses. The next morning was Wednesday and the girls got off to school when I picked them up in the morning. They went home to change and shower and when they had to go home first, it was an early start to the day. They were up by six a.m. and at school by seven-thirty. The bell sounded and they left homeroom for their studies. Blakely's day was the same every day as it was for every high school student, but in the evenings, she changed it up a bit. Blake was also starting lacrosse soon. That day in Latin, Shay talked about homecoming with some of the other girls as if Blakely wasn't even there. It was high school, and it wasn't cool to be friends with anyone outside the squad.

When the third bell rang for the day, Blakely was off to lunch. She was without Mike and the girls cooed like school children.

"Where's the boy toy?" Kennedy chided from the balcony.

Blakely was already seated.

The nerd brigade sat at the table next to her and because the popular girls had spoken it was the cool thing to do – to gawk and snigger. Blakely felt truly embarrassed, and she took paper out of her pack to begin a letter. She truly needed her friend in that moment. She

184

wrote to Tamara who she never got to see because they were on two opposite ends of the spectrum: Tamara was a dirt-poor farm girl and Blakely was from an average income family in the burbs. They had two different brains: Tamara was right brained and creative (hence her passion for Jewel's sense of style) while Blakely was predominately left brained girl who was proficient in the straight-A category, but she loved English. She loved writing letters even if she couldn't write better than Tamara – which they had in common. Tamara had beautiful handwriting and often misspelled, and Blakely would have fared better as an editor, while Tamara was the creator of lavish stories. She could write in detail about faraway places. Blakely kept her writing mostly at home base.

Her letter writing didn't dissuade the Kennedy clique, however.

"You look like a toad with ears," Kennedy's boyfriend Eric jested from the bottom floor. Their lunch cafeteria reminded Blakely of prison-like tiers if it had bars. She felt tight and claustrophobic like the walls were caving in. So, she started another letter. That one to Chad. She confided to him in that letter everything the cool ones were saying to her. That way it was as though she had a friend. She didn't intend to mail the letter but intended to hand deliver because she could tell him anything. He made her feel that comfortable. Even Tamara had been distant lately. She was working a lot and Blakely knew she was trying to save the farm. Blakely tried to help her, too. She wasn't sure if she wanted it or was appreciated but that's because Tamara had an ego and she was too proud – she and her brothers, close as their DNA, were the heroes over their father's farm, especially since their mother left. Blakely took her two letters in her hand and left the table, despite the bellowing from down below, and left her tray sitting at the table so she wouldn't have to undergo the humiliation of Kennedy and Eric and their friends. When she got to the top tier of her prison, she found Tamara and handed her the letter, when she heard the terrible scrutiny from behind.

"Aren't you going to take your tray down or just leave it for someone else?" Kennedy's voice echoed.

"You didn't take down your tray?" Tamara wasn't helpful.

Blakely took off. Down the hall. Away. Away from them and the taunting words that echoed in her brain through biology ,where she didn't find Mike because he probably skipped that day, instead of the alternative of lunch detention. Certainly, he had to have known they would get to him and detention would be unavoidable.

Chapter Sixteen

The following day was Friday and we ditched school because we were heading off to Florida a day early, before the actual beginning of Labor Day weekend: the school was closed Monday and Tuesday. We would be in Florida for four days. There were no available flights, so we drove thirteen hours there Thursday night and thirteen hours back on Tuesday. It was worth it. Me, Adam, and Blake went in my Jeep, while Diesel and Sherry went in her Jeep. The girls would drive. We went Jeeping with the soft roof off and the wind in our hair. Straight down 95 south ... all the way there without rain. Our first day there – rain. But we were beat and stayed in the hotel anyway. But not Blakely. She had other plans. She grabbed a flyer that advertised what to do while staying in Florida. She scanned the headlines and saw a performance being held at an indoor theater. She went out without asking – but who was I to tell her no? – and her first stop was the restaurant where he worked. She got seated alone. She sat and waited and then turned beet red. He held her favorite yellow roses in his hand and presented them to her. He anticipated her visit since his last letter. It was late. She was fourteen. We were in Florida together, and she was meeting a boy. Chad made her quiver with excitement. His dark hair, dark eyes, and dark nature were so alluring to her. She was love struck and he really was handsome.

He sat down across from her – she showed up there on the hour he got off from a long shift. But he had energy for Blakely. He looked tired but his demeanor was upbeat.

"How are you, Angel?" he said with light in his eyes.

"Angel?" She relished the compliment.

"That's what I think of you." He was genuine. "You're like an angel that's found me here in Florida … I mean, all the way from Virginia."

"I know." Her voice was soft. "I thought about that, too. Like, what are the odds of finding you here?"

They made small talk after that. About what had been going on in their lives for the past week. They chatted over salad and toast. He extended his hand to her, and she felt comforted by his touch.

"There are some girls who don't like me."

He wasn't surprised.

"People are unfair to other people."

"Yes. I know. You are right."

She thought of what it meant to be his people and the period of history known as The Trail of Tears, and she smiled at his knowing hardship and to still exude kindness. He was gentle really, but his physique was strong. It was a great balance. A complement in his identity.

"Where would you like to go?" He paid the bill.

She then felt dumb because she had earned enough cash and could help, "I'll get the next tab." She wanted to be equals.

"Next tab?"

"How about the theater?" she said.

"Okay. Sure."

They wanted to see a gory film. They didn't know the other had a thing for horror movies. It was perfect. She screamed into his neck. He smelled of cologne and sweat. Another great balance in his physique and his demeanor; he smelled so masculine but could scream into his armpit. He squeezed her hand. They held hands through all of it. Through the blood curdling screaming and angst. The end was a great resolve to the demise; the protagonist didn't know how she would see through it all. Through the hell she was undergoing. There was a bitter, small light of hope, and then there was none until something unlikely happened and there was solace. The nightmare would be over for the moment in the cliffhanger at the end. Chad confided to her that he wanted to write movies. That he wanted to study theater and film in college. He confided that he had been working extra shifts. That his grades were at times mediocre at best, but he wanted to climb the corporate ladder in the realm of television. He earned what he needed at the restaurant.

Chad would be sixteen at the start of the following year and he talked about how much he would like to see her. He said how he could visit Virginia more; he wanted to travel; he was already a man of sorts. He had a job, and he scored his own set of wheels. He had his learners permit, but didn't want to ruin getting his official license by driving out of bounds or outside the rules. He had his father and he had Sedgwick, too. He thought going to Virginia for the holiday was an option.

"Do you celebrate Christmas?" she said without hope.

"Not on the reservation," was his response, and she could understand that Christmas wasn't on the regime of the Creek.

"But you would like to visit me?"

"Of course." He was sincere.

She looked him in the eye, and he looked back at her. He placed a generous hand to her left cheek, and they kissed subtly on the lips in an embrace that deserves a first kiss. He walked with her into the night at the beach. The sun was setting, and I admittedly started to worry about her. They took off their sneakers and flops and walked in the sand that had begun to cool. It felt good between their toes. She asked him about television, and he did some pretty impressive John Wayne and

190

Jackie Chan impressions. He could do voices of popular film cinematography, too. He wanted to act but he also wanted to produce. He could write, too; he explained to her that he had original ideas for a good TV pilot but he mostly wanted to do film. He wanted to study theater there in Florida. Blakely told him of her passion for animals and how she'd like to help rescues care for their fosters. Her grades were stellar enough for her to study veterinary science and she seemed serious about it.

"It's what I've decided on fairly recently," she told him.

Blake wasn't sure where exactly she fit in, although she was pretty good at almost every subject in high school. Sherry and I wanted to take off to Florida since our freshman year of high school. The stars seemed to align that way for Blakely, too. She went with him until it turned midnight, then she showed up at the hotel. She didn't have to sneak in. I was up.

"How was the theater?" I said not wanting to sound uncool.

"It was good." She was nonchalant.

"Blake," I said determined, "what were you really doing?"

"What do you mean? I really went to the theater."

"What did you see?" Now I was being uncool.

"A total slasher movie." She went to the bathroom

191

and shut the door.

I was beginning to see how hard it was to parent. She really had me concerned. I went to bed.

In the morning she was already gone with a note left on the table.

I'm fine. The handwriting was elegant, I'm going to the beach.

The four of us, Diesel, Sherry and Adam, hopped in my Jeep and we went out to scour the beach.

Blakely was always a quiet one. She kept most things to herself. I didn't really know what to think but I was catching on that she wasn't there to hang out with us, and I was fairly certain she wasn't spending all her time alone – or was she? I knew Blake was independent and strong willed, but I truly felt I should check on her.

The beach was busy and looking for Blakely was like looking for a grain of sand among the thousands. She wasn't going to be visible. I got scared. I thought of all the ways of being kidnapped. I was at my lowest, feeling shamed for taking her there just so she could run away.

I didn't know Chad had taken her to see Sedgwick in a band, which scored a gig at the restaurant affront the beach. I was never going to find her. Sedgwick sang in a band and played lead guitar. He had a great deal of talent. His band Aerospace played some covers and then he got to sing a few songs he wrote. He played acoustic while giving his band a break, and then he took the break and let the band backup sing a few songs. He wasn't bad. His name was Marcus Scott, and he sang well enough, but didn't quite have the vocal cords Sedgwick had. Marcus started the band just into high school and they played locally and were well known. Blakely didn't know the restaurant off the beach could house live entertainment, but they opened the back wall which led right to the sand, the water, and the sun. It was dine-in or dine-out and one could still hear the live entertainment.

Then I saw her. They were holding hands and walked to the pier overlooking a brilliant sunset after the few hours of entertainment, food, and fun ended.

"Blakely," I said from the Jeep.

"Oh, hey," she really wasn't amused.

"Who's your friend?" I was being cool and composed from sheer relief.

Adam exited the Jeep.

Blakely approached him. "Be cool," she said, "he is really important to me."

Adam kept his cool, too.

"Hey man," Adam tossed his hand for a shake and Chad was super smooth.

"Hey, what's happening?" he said with a smile.

193

"Not much. Just went looking for Blakely after she dipped out on us."

"Wait," he said to Blakely, "didn't you tell them where you were going?"

She shrugged, "The beach." She was brief.

"Bro," Diesel yelled from the ride, "you all want to go check out some local hot spots?"

Sherry and Diesel were into motorcycles, and it happened to be bike week.

"I don't mind." Chad seemed up for anything.

"No, thanks," Blakely wasn't into it, "bikers and gangs aren't my thing."

"They should be." Diesel wasn't fazed.

"Yeah, hell, why not?" Chad nudged her shoulder as Sedgwick came to meet up with them.

"What's going down?" Sedgwick looked confident. "We haven't been introduced…" he was right.

"Oh, sorry," a now shy Blakely turned toward us. "This is my sister and her friends."

"Does your sister have a name?" He was still smiling.

"Vanessa." She was candid.

194

"I'm Adam. Her boyfriend."

"I'm Chad…" he began but was interrupted.

"How did you all meet?" Adam was intrusive and I saw Blakely's face.

"In Virginia. At the reservoir."

"Really? When?"

"A couple months ago." Blakely really looked like she wanted to run.

"Well, hey, you all want to hang with us for a while?" Adam wasn't really asking.

"Of course." Chad was interested in knowing us. I could tell.

There wasn't any more room in my ride, so Sedgwick was given an address and we met up at a spot where everyone with bikes liked to congregate. At the same venue there were a team of crotch rockets where their riders were being chill. They appealed to Blakely more. Perhaps she could relate to them. Then a brigade of muscle cars showed. The place was vintage and the girls and guys who served there were in roller skates. We never saw anything like it back home. The place was also kind of contemporary with a flare like a diner on steroids. It was massive and on the top floor, out on the roof, there was a restaurant and more live entertainment. Sedgwick knew the band members. He told us the band was a chick band called The Mermaids – a punk rock band with some

195

hipster young women who could play; the lead singer was striking with fire engine red hair, piercings, and tattoos. They were the perfect band for the place. He said the lead singer, Sadie, and Marcus used to date. Blakely seemed to relax a little and she ordered a mango tea, and we had some pub chips and beer cheese. The place wasn't going to serve minors, of course, so we were there to eat and hear the music.

The place was alive with punk rock, bikers, and brew, but we got to sit outside by the sunset and chat when Sadie took a break and met up with Sedgwick. Evidently, she had a thing for him, but he wasn't into dating an ex of one of his best friends. She didn't know Chad though so as she got to know him, I got to know him, too. Chad had a quiet life on the reservation until his dad scored a gig building boats in Florida. He attended regular public schools and got to know a diverse array of citizens and many tourists; his restaurant was a tourist hot spot. I learned all that I could about the guy, especially since my younger sister took an interest in him and I had never seen her interested in anyone before.

Diesel was highly interested in the motor heads, as he called them and himself. They rode choppers and chatted about fixing cars. Sherry was also into learning about Chad, so we let our guys mosey around a bit after the gist was on the table. Chad didn't seem like a guy who harbored deep secrets, but I was second guessing Blakely's harboring of dark secrets. But the cat was out of the bag. I thought Adam would lose interest after the guy was thought to be genuine. They were free to go do their own thing while Sherry and I went back to the hotel without the guys so we could go for a swim in the pool.

Chad and Blakely left the biker bar and went for a stroll down the beach. They just liked one another, and it showed. I met Adam when I was fourteen and Dad was just too busy to keep a leash on us. Mom partied and didn't dare intrude if we stayed out of her hair. As the day turned to night and the moon was waning to a new moon, Chad took Blakely to one more spot while the rest of us did our own thing; he took her out on one of his father's boat. It turned out that Chad was highly nautical and maneuvered that port with sense and sophistication. It was out on that boat where Blakely saw a family of dolphins; that was the first time she opened up about us as a family, or the lack of one, and Chad listened as she spoke. She told him about Samira, her mother Alisa, and her dating Dad. She said she liked Samira, her mom, her boyfriend Jared, and her best friend Simone. She said Simone was dating Billy, and Herb and Alex were lovers and she sounded down a tad.

"Why the voice?" He was tender.

"What voice?" she said softly.

"You sound really upset. Or shaken?"

"I found you ..." she paused "and you're so far away."

"And they all have each other?" He totally got her.

"Yes," she said.

"I'll be down for Christmas." He was sweet. "It'll be here before you know it."

"I guess." She stayed somber in the moment as they chatted on a boat in the Florida Bay as a family of dolphins was illuminated by the light of the moon.

He kissed her subtly on the forehead and the purple sky turned black. Then Chad took Blakely home.

Chapter Seventeen

We drove home on Tuesday. After a thirteen-hour drive, we crashed into our beds with our faces in our pillows; we begrudgingly returned to high school the next morning, when the middle of the week should not feel like a Monday. But feeling like the middle of the week didn't fare much better. So, we all began to concentrate more on Homecoming than the beginning of exams.

"Who are you going with?" Chrissy Lane chided from behind.

Mike sat slumped and awkward in his chair.

He knew his brother, who was only a year older, liked the girl he sat next to in biology.

"Are they lesbians?" Rob scoured.

"Yes. Don't you know?" Chrissy was seemingly being serious, but Blakely didn't care what they thought about her and Tamara.

"Shay and Chris are official." Chrissy was gloating.

No one really understood why Blakely and Tamara didn't have boyfriends, so the rumor spread that they were lesbians. They didn't care and minded their own business as much as possible.

"Are you going?" Blakely finally said to Mike.

"No." He was frank.

He knew Joe wanted to ask Tamara and he thought about asking Blakely, but he just didn't. No one will ever know why.

That Friday night was Homecoming and Blakely and Tamara decided to go together.

"Isn't it sad how many people don't have a date?" Shay chided the next day, Thursday, in Latin class, seated next to Chris. Blakely decided Shay was only dating Chris instead of Jeremy because they sat together in Latin.

Rumor had it that Jeremy asked Shay discretely, but she broke it to him that Chris beat him to it. Whatever the case was, the pair was then official. Jeremy was class clown and never serious. It would be difficult seeing him paired with a girl who had that much control to deal with all his shenanigans.

"He's just goofy," Shay said to Chris, and Chris shrugged.

Shay was gorgeous and had the wealth paired with her gifted genes.

It was true, however, that the entire cheer squad had a date and they all marveled over one another.

Jeremy's personality made him friends with everybody, but dateable to none. But perhaps he was also the type to go with a non-cheer girl. Blakely mused over it all momentarily until the bell rang and she went on to lunch and classes without the thought of not having a date and the entire school thinking they were lesbians (in their defense – so what if they were?)

Blakely worked that Friday night. The doors opened for Homecoming at nine o'clock and Blakely, Tamara, Cherish, Lacy, and Skye worked until ten. They got in Cherish's car with the windows down, British indie pop blaring from the speakers, and they met with their guys as the happiest not-so-popular kids on the block. Cherish with Jason, Lacy with David, and Skye with Archie, entered the building. Inside they would not find Frankie or Kurt, who went to a different school and had their own Homecoming. Tamara took Blakely into her arms, and they played the scene the gossip and rumors were all about. They held hands and Blakely sat between her legs and crossed one leg over hers.

It was Jeremy who beat everyone to it.

"That's a fine-looking sandwich," he bellowed across the hall. Archie, Jason, and David rose from their chairs.

"Wouldn't mind getting between those two slices of bread…" he bit his knuckles.

"How about I give you a knuckle sandwich?" Jason was floored.

"How about you be completely unoriginal?" Jeremy was as smart as he was dumb. He walked off. The music played and the floor was consumed with bodies. They slow-danced and had their photos taken. They were happy in the company of each another.

"I'm planning a party for the twinsies," Cherish said as the music played and Lacy and Skye danced with their partners.

"Where?" Blakely really didn't need to ask.

Rick's place was a primary location for underage drinking parties where the cops hadn't found out about it.

Cherish confirmed her suspicion.

Rick's place had the pool and outdoor amenities. They just needed to supply the food and music.

Then the Kennedy crew appeared, and Blakely felt nervous; they stared her down like a dog does a mouse – like carnivorous things with teeth. They all just stared: Kennedy and Jason, her bestie Jessica and her date Mason, Vivian Clancy and Troy Matthews, Angel and Tyler, and Shay with Chris – the entire cheer squad and half the football team were a gauntlet of trouble for Blakely and a summation of clichés – but it didn't matter – they were the popular ones. The ones everyone else would want to be. They had rich cars. Fine houses. Huge wealth. And gorgeous physiques. They were the Stanton in-crowd, and they were staring at Blakely and her crew like a dog does meat – and they were the little people. They were the nice ones.

"Ewww, Jeremy," Kennedy bellowed loud enough for all to hear. "You'd be desperate for those two," she chided and he scoffed.

"I'd be happy." He didn't care.

"Gross." Kennedy winced.

Almost the entire Stanton student body was now staring in their direction. Then the music stopped, and they could hear one another speak.

"Who wants to get out of here?" a voice said from behind.

"What the hell?" Jason said. "Who let you in here?"

It was Frankie alongside Kurt.

"We're here to rescue your asses," Frankie laughed.

It was going on midnight by the time they showed, and the dance was ending.

"It's about time, bro," Jason said, and they fist bumped. Archie and David took their ladies by the hand, and they walked out into the night to get some late night food, and the only place they knew was serving until two a.m. It was Denny's and it was crowded inside. The girls sat down in their dresses and ordered Cokes with steamed vegetables and cheese over fries. They didn't keep it light. The food was heavy, but it filled their famished stomachs. They liked the plant protein that kept their merits merry.

"What had to die for you to eat that?" Cherish cooed.

"A fucking hippopotamus," Jason choked down his burger.

Cherish lightly pushed his shoulder.

"What?" He was into meat.

The girls weren't.

Kurt and Frankie asked about the dance, to which they replied, "It was okay."

Then walked in Joe, who refused to go to the dance.

Tamara squeezed beside Blakely as Joe scooted into the cushion. They were shoulder to shoulder.

"How's Mike?" Blakely was genuinely interested.

"He's out with a girl," is all Joe would offer.

"Oh? Who?" Blakely was genuinely curious as well.

"Some girl named Sam."

204

"Wait." Blakely paused. "Does she work at a hotel? Reception?"

"Yeah, something like that." Joe waved in a waitress, "Can I get a menu?"

He was late. Kurt set up the time for all of them to be there.

Joe ordered a platter of breakfast. "Nothing like kegs and eggs," he said when his meal arrived.

The rest were finished, and they talked about where to crash for the night. It was obvious they would be going to Kurt's apartment. Archie and David had also settled in nicely and they still referred to is as Kurt's place until he reminded them it was then our apartment. The crew felt too cool for school having their own place. The girls enjoyed having a place to crash. The Basement was still a hang out too, but the apartment was their go-to for beer, bong hits, parties, and more. They cozied on the couch and played quarters, a round of asshole, some spades, and poker. It wasn't strip poker that time as they all got enough of Frankie's nudity the last time they all hung out together. The parties were simple enough and they were never too loud, and the cops were never called. Blakely was comfortable enough, but she missed Chad, and a week after Labor Day weekend she got a postcard in the mail along with a delivery of fresh cut yellow roses – her favorite.

She took the roses, the post card, and a letter to her room, and she opened an envelope that also contained some photos – he went all out that time. She settled into bed, glad that the letter came as early as it had because that meant he was thinking about her as much as she was thinking about him. The next day started the week off at school, the day all the kids got their photos from Homecoming. Blakely saw the girls down the tier below mingle over portraits of themselves, and gossip about who had the best dress. For Blakely it was like being at Homecoming all over again; the girls were loud, and their piercing voices echoed from across the room. Kennedy was giddy over Eric, who was crowded by buddies who were in their football jerseys – football was starting and they had a new coach. Coach Green was a menace on the field, and he took no crap from his team. They had practice that day after school and the cheer squad was also aiming to be ready for the opening game scheduled that Friday – a home game, and Bell was their adversary.

The night began in a smooth tone of admiration and awe. Stanton kids lined up at the gates for an opening game that was peaceful, serene, and calm. I sat in the bleachers beside Adam, Sherry, and Diesel. Samira along with her partner Jared and their friends Simone and Billy, and Herb and Alex, sat on the bleachers below. The Kennedy squad and their boyfriends decorated the field. Tamara surprised Blakely by showing up; Tony let her go an hour early since the crowd wasn't there that night; instead, the town showed for opening football against the biggest rival in high school history – Bell High kids were loud in the bleachers.

The ref appeared and flung the quarter high in the air and the away team fans cheered – Bell would be starting offense. Kennedy and her team cheered on... Go team go, could be heard from the voices of all the pretty girls, and Stanton formed a line-up as the first punt was made – a Bell lineman made a pass and secured their quarterback, Chris Kelley, who watched as Bell made what seemed like an easy first down. By the time the first half was finished, and they retreated to their locker room for half time, Stanton was down by a touchdown; that fact didn't stop the cheer team who kept the Stanton fans optimistic, and they secured the place with real team spirit. It was hard on Blakely being hated by Kennedy. She truly never did anything to her. But she didn't have to. Kennedy had it out for her out of pure unadulterated hatred; she was Kennedy's nemesis by choice. Blakely could pass a test with flying colors; she was gifted smart. Kennedy was gifted in the way of commodities and that alone made her very popular.

The Stanton football team re-emerged as the half time show ended, and Blakely could feel the hairs stand on the back of her neck as Bell scored another touchdown and Stanton was losing into the third. Blakely could feel the hatred almost emanating from every one of those players as myself and Simone and all our friends cheered on and Stanton, Blakely among them, were on the losing end.

"Why don't you just go hang out over there where you belong," sneered a voice from the edge of the field, and Blakely was horrified to find Shay rolling her eyes as Chris fumbled the ball that was intercepted by Bell in the fourth quarter. The Stanton jerks knew me and Simone from the reservoir parties, and the stand-off between Stanton and Bell was felt among us. Blakely was on their turf for the sake of her best friend, and Tamara rubbed her back to say it would be okay. But it wouldn't be okay. And Blakely knew it because she felt it and every hair on her body stood up.

Bell beat Stanton despite a field goal kick in the end that would not win the game for Stanton: twenty-one to seventeen. Bell students and fans cheered from the stands as Stanton kids walked off the field defeated. And that's exactly how Blakely would feel, because she was the kid who by territory didn't belong there.

It was a rough next day as Tamara and Blakely began work Saturday morning with Tamara working the cook top for the coffee shop and Blakely along with her girls Cherish, Lacy, and Skye, who were not at the game, were caught up with what went down.

"We had to be here," Cherish said as Lacy and Skye agreed.

"Tony wouldn't let us go," Lacy sighed.

"Was the place even busy?" Blakely asked as she hastily poured soda from the fountain.

"No, he was on a kick about cleaning this place."

Tony knew the crowd would be in following a

football game and he was right.

The Stanton crowd flooded through the doors at opening for some of the best breakfast in town – and they were there to talk about the game. The coffee shop was full, and no seat was left empty in the dining room either.

"It was hard to lose," one man said to Chris Matthews' mother who was there with some girlfriends because the men were busy on the field. Stanton had practice on Saturdays. Tamara and Blakely worked a double shift on both Saturday and Sunday, and they ended up both going home after a long weekend of knowing the other was too tired.

They survived the weekend to end up at school the next day. A terrible Monday and everyone was moody; the weather outside was a disaster with wind and rain. Then it happened. Blakely stepped into the cafeteria with her tray held between both hands and she placed one foot on the step and felt a pain in her left ankle as Kennedy faced her, and Blakely went face first into her plate and went down onto a tray of pasta and sauce. The entire cafeteria erupted into laughter. Blakely stood with pasta sauce down her face, onto her clothes, and down her legs. It covered the front of her like mud on an animal.

"Look at the pig covered in sauce!" Kennedy added to the humiliation.

"You tripped me." Blakely's voice was soft.

"Prove it." Kennedy didn't back off.

"Why don't you run to your little friends," Jessica, the typically reserved and shy one said to the left of Kennedy.

"Or go home crying to your mom," Chrissy, who hardly knew Blakely at all, said from the right.

They walked off, leaving Blakely covered in spaghetti while those in the cafeteria mostly turned back to their own plates.

Mike wasn't in school that day. At least he wasn't anywhere to be found.

Blakely walked off up toward the top floor without a single bite to eat.

"What the hell happened to her?" One guy said to the other and they turned to look but Blakely, with her book bag still on her back, turned to the office and placed her letter in the outgoing basket.

"Blakely, my word, what happened to you dear?" Mrs. Dempsey said from behind the counter.

"I fell in my, I fell in my spaghetti." Her voice was flat. She wasn't completely shaken.

She exited onto the top floor of the cafeteria with twenty-five minutes remaining for her lunch period, knowing the Kennedy crew was in the bathroom, so she dared not enter the hall, which was forbidden between

210

classes, and went to the girl's room where she entered the stall not knowing what to do.

Chapter Eighteen

Blakely was numb. After removing as much of the sauce as she could, she left the school grounds. She didn't ask the teacher and she didn't talk to anyone in the office. She just left. It took her hours to walk home, but that's what she did. She then went to work. A pizza stain on her shirt was a gauge in the eye, too – just another reminder of the stains on her beloved shirt. She tenderly tried to salvage the shirt, but the red sauce stained the white satin. She took to the restroom in the restaurant and feverishly tried to wash the stain from her work shirt before it set in.

Then Mom walked through the front door as Blakely was making an exit from the restroom.

"Oh Blakely, I'm so sorry," she cried.

Blakely wondered how her mother could hear the news so fast.

"It's okay, Mom." She withdrew away from her. "It was just some sauce. Nothing to get hysterical over."

Mom's face went cold. "No, honey," she said calmly, "I'm not sure what you're talking about..."

Then Steve made an appearance.

"It's your friend, Mike..." Mom was sullen.

"He's been in an accident." Steve was trying to be supportive.

"What are you talking about?"

Blakely already had enough for one day.

"Sam called us."

"She told us that Mike was your friend…" Mom added.

"Mike is down the road here, Blake." Steve was still trying out his role as stepdad. Blakely couldn't fathom what those two bird brains were trying to tell her; Mom was trying to play her role too, then, as a mother after all the years as an absent person in her life as early as age eleven – Blakey didn't want to hear their shit. She wasn't amused.

She scoffed, "Just what the hell are you two talking about?"

That's when Cherish made her entrance and appeared morose.

"Blakely," she put her arms around her. "I'm so sorry."

She still wasn't processing the news.

"It's Mike, your Mike, Joe's brother…"

Her words trailed off as Blakely began to feel

213

claustrophobic. "What?" She wasn't prepared for the news.

"He…"

Cherish couldn't get the words out.

They told Blakely that Mike was killed in a Mazda Miata that was wrapped around a tree less than a half mile down the street from The Pub. He was still in the car. Wrapped around the tree. Mike was approached by his cousin who wanted to take the Miata for a test drive; he drove too fast around a sharp bend and crashed into, around, a large oak tree. Mike was in the passenger seat. Cherish saw him take his last breath as she got out of the car before the responders arrived; Cherish found Mike in his last moment sitting in the passenger seat of a Mazda Miata with his side of the vehicle smashed while his cousin was unscathed.

Blakely returned home that evening knowing she would prepare for his funeral that would likely be that weekend, so she took out some paper and began a letter:

Dear Chad,

Today is one of the worst days of my life …

Her letter began, and she sulked quietly in her room as she wrote the letter until she couldn't keep her eyes open any longer. In the morning, Sam made an appearance at Blakely's home. Samira opened the door as it was her week to stay with Alisa. Sam entered and found a sullen Blakely who still held onto a tissue, still trying to process that Mike, her loyal friend and best buddy – her only buddy – at the lunch table – was gone from this world.

"He read the letter," Sam began to explain, "that Shay wrote Chrissy." She paused, "They planned to do some really nasty things to you."

"What do you mean?"

"Mike didn't want to tell you… he planned to stop them if they dared to hurt you."

"Tell me what it said."

"Mike didn't want to hurt you…"

"Tell me what it said." Blakely felt nothing. She went numb again.

"They called you a pig in a trough…"

"That's it?"

"Something about being covered in waste like a swine…"

"I don't think you should be saying this right now." Samira looked to Blakely.

"No, I'm fine. What else did they say?"

"They we're going to smash your face into the lunch tray… if you walked past their table one more

215

time … acting like you think you're cute."

"I think I'm cute?"

"I thought you should know because if Mike had been there, he would have protected you."

"How do you know…?"

"Mike heard from Joe. Then he told us both what happened to you in the cafeteria. The entire school talked about it. Bell even knows."

"Yeah, I heard it, too. The bus." Samira explained. "Some of the kids who showed up at Bell for practice before a game said what happened. Simone was on cheer and told me later, on the bus." Samira looked hurt for some-day-to-be stepsister.

"Thanks for coming." Blakely told Sam who was a cute and petite girl who worked evening reception at the resort; the night shift went to day shift and Sam took over at night. Blakely learned that Mike and Joe's Uncle Porter was staying at the resort for a golf tournament, and when he went to visit his uncle he met Sam. They hit it off fast; Sam explained that Mike was sweet and asked for her number. They chatted during her lunch break, and he eventually mentioned Blakely; they eventually put it together that Blakely was the resort owner's daughter. Blakely corrected her saying "step-daughter" because she was in no way connected to Steve.

The world became too small and too coincidental

when Cherish and Donna drove past an accident that beheld her best guy friend who died in that moment less than a mile from Blakely's employment, on a night she had been working. She got herself ready and went off to school, not knowing what the day would bring. It was beyond them to feel remorse for Blakely in the face of losing her best friend. They didn't dare speak a word of it and went on in their lives like nothing had happened; Blakely was appalled that Kennedy and her crew had the nerve to show up at the viewing later that evening to mourn a Stanton student they hardly got to know.

She took a step toward the casket and knelt beside him with angst in her soul, "You were there," she said, and she kissed his cheek and the tears rolled from her face. She knew Mike a few short months, but she felt close to him when he sat beside her at lunch and biology. She had biology again and again – a shallow reminder of the warm body that used to sit next to her. She saw Joe. He was inoculated with booze. No one dared to scorn him. At night, the Stanton kids and Samira's clique gathered at his fresh grave; mud was abundant where he was laid, and flowers were tipped over to cover the mush that was his permanent resting place. Blakely sobbed. She made it all the way to November when Cherish brought up the twinsies' party again. She hadn't forgotten but she didn't have it in her, honestly. Even Donna went back to life. They were all able to go back to life. Blakely was split in two between Florida and Virginia. She sat down to write another letter, this time during a much-needed break from work, inside the coffee shop, at a corner table where it was dark and secluded. Her inner world had truly

217

turned dark because Mike was a protector, a friend, and a damn nice person. He lit the room with incandescence. She wrote furiously. She had little time. In a short forty-five minutes she was called from the dining room because some guests were seated, an hour after opening, and Blakely was the server on duty. Cherish was there as hostess and to bus tables. She poured the drinks and at the end of the night they split the tips. Cherish mentioned Lacy and Skye again to Blakely hoping to get a rise out of her. She couldn't. But Blakely kept going through the night despite wanting the world to stop or to at least slow down.

The next day of school was cold. The autumn leaves had changed, had fallen, had blown away, until the bare-naked branches whistled in the wind. The Stanton kids had seen four losses and three victories – it was the year the streak ended. The cool kids weren't keeping their cool. They were furious to be beaten by Bell twice and it added to the pressure of the rivalry between the two schools. Blakely sat at a lunch table alone. She cried some and she mostly ate very slowly and deliberately to force something into her stomach. She yearned for the bell and when it sounded, she met Tamara in passing and gave her letter and the other she deposited into the outgoing basket. Blakely returned to biology where Chrissy dared to snigger, and Blakely turned a cold shoulder – she was permanently numb since the day her friend was taken from her a mere quarter of a mile from where she was, as though it was there to taunt her every time she went to work. Just like lunch. Just like biology.

She wondered how much his cousin suffered who had been like Joe; they drank to wash their pain, to drown it in whiskey, to make the gaping hole feel somehow filled. She quit her job. It was coming to an end for Blakely. She quit on a Friday night and the next day she went shopping for Lacy and Skye so that she could at least show her face in a social kind of way. She purchased socks, perfume, and lip gloss. They put it in a cute candied decorated bag and added the tissue paper. Next, she got birthday cards. She got gag gifts. She needed a laugh because most of the time she wanted to scream. To wail at the top of her lungs. She wanted cold, hard sarcasm so she could punch it in the face. Point blank: Blakely was conflicted between love for life and pure hatred.

That evening she read a letter from Chad. He had small talk to say and was overall still joyful about planning to see her the next month for Christmas. She had already sent a letter that day, so she went to bed early. That weekend she did not see Tamara or any of her other friends. Sherry and I stopped our work routine to check on her and to offer her a job; retail was busy during the holidays, and she could continue to save up money for the new Jeep she always wanted. Blakely didn't want a job there. She didn't want a job anywhere; what she wanted was a break. She got it. She had three weeks off and then it was Lacy and Skye's birthday bash at Rick's place. Blakely hadn't been to The Basement, Kurt's apartment, the pool hall, or The Rock at all in the last three weeks. She heard from no one. She seemed nearly completely shut down.

She arrived at the party by taxi, which was me and Adam, and she went inside. We took off. She had told us that we didn't need to pick up Tamara because her brothers had already dropped her off. Tamara found the whole crew there, even Joe. But he was intoxicated, as that had become his norm after the death of his brother. Rick was there to supply the party pad while the rest were there to B.Y.O.B (bring your own beer) and the host of the house, Cherish and David, supplied the kegs. The party had a DJ; it looked like the party they had a few months back for Tamara. August was much hotter than November, of course, so Lacy and Skye's party was held in the basement. The DJ played from the theater room. The house was big. Immaculate. And the Stanton kids could throw a party like they partied hard. The turn of the millennium was soon to give way to another year. But first they had cold beer and bongs to fill.

Blakely found Tamara who was watching Frankie and Kurt face off for the fastest one who could bong forty ounces of malt liquor. It was a day to puke, Blakely thought. They had Crown Royal, Smirnoff, Captain Morgan, Jim Beam, Jameson … the alcohol was high end. They had a bar set up in the basement. Kids poured in like twenty-one year olds flood the bars – house parties were for high school kids back in the hay-day. There were leather sofas and marble tables. Cherish didn't come from an as-prosperous family, but her mother's brother operated the electric company. Blakely tapped Tamara on the shoulder, but Tamara didn't turn around until it was pointed out to her by Joe that Blakely wanted her attention.

Tamara then whirled around, "What," she said. Blakely was embarrassed momentarily and didn't know what to think.

"I'm here," Blakely said.

"Yeah, so? You're here. That's great." Tamara turned her back again and Blakely devised a plan.

"Tam, can you come with me please?" Blakely took her by the hand, and they went to the nearest bathroom as Cherish followed behind them. The three of them went inside. Cherish took down her jeans and had to pee. Tamara found that the door would not lock and commanded Blakely to watch the door.

"Go stand in front of the door," she yelled.

"No…" Blakely didn't care about the door in that moment.

"I said go block the door…" Tamara grabbed Blakely and threw her into the door. Blakely fell to the floor with her back to the door.

Cherish laughed. She was drunk. But it hurt.

Blakely felt lost and confused.

Tamara stood in front of her and didn't lift a finger to help her. Blakely knew she had been distant since Mike's death, but she couldn't understand Tam's behavior or her obvious disdain.

221

Blakely finally got to her feet. She stood her ground. Then Tamara shoved her way through the door and made an exit. It seemed obvious that Blakely had become unfriended.

"What's her problem?" she asked Cherish who was hiking up her pants.

"I don't flipping know." She had also smoked weed.

Blakely walked through the door and found Tamara sitting on the sofa and she tried again to just talk to her most beloved friend.

"Tam…" her voice trailed off as Blakely stood beside her and Tamara propped her feet up on the marble table which cracked beneath her feet and split in half, sending the table crashing onto the floor. Blakely gasped. Tamara stood up and moved to the adjacent room where Rick was shooting pool. She followed after to find Tamara over Rick – explaining how Blakely had just broken the table. Blakely didn't enter the room. She was too abashed to reason with her. She left the party and never got to see if Lacy or Skye liked the gifts.

Chapter Nineteen

Blakely begrudgingly returned to school following the biggest party the school ever had. All of Stanton had been there; they weren't sober in lieu of finally scoring another win that tied them four and four. They still had a month of the season. It was cold and they still played hard. The Stanton Mustangs were a football team of tremendous athletes and they blamed having a new coach for falling out of the winning streak. But Coach Brown also brought them up; he had a way with words, and he was furious on the field. He upped the practices, and he went full charge that following Friday to play for the last time against Bell for that season. The school had a pep rally planned to motivate the kids as they got ready to play against Bell. The Cheer team was furious about new routines and the high school band brought together their greatest talents the school ever had; then the football jocks were fully charged and pumped to get to Friday.

Then there was my sister, who sat alone at the table with five empty chairs and zero friends close by. Blakely Elizabeth O'Connor was out of her league within a school where she didn't have jurisdiction and was attending on a forged note. Blakely was called into the office to find Donna there, who stood over a forged note.

"Blakely dear," Mrs. Dempsey said, who liked Blakely a lot, "you left a note in the basket without an address or even a stamp." Mrs. Dempsey handed Blakely a note with the attention to Tamara and it dawned on her that she had in fact placed Tamara's note into the outgoing basket meaning the note she gave Tamara was for Chad.

Tamara had Chad's letter.

It further dawned on her that Tamara must have ratted her out to the school, and she found her suspicion was correct when she got called into the principles' office because he didn't care to be frank: "Ms. Day informed the school counselor that your daughter was attending Stanton on a forged letter."

Blakely felt as though she were smacked in the face.

She went out of her way to unfriend Blakely because she liked a boy. But Tamara did her a favor because Blake didn't need to be there anymore. Then Mom came to Dad's and found Alisa, who had mostly moved in, which worked in Mom's favor because she could then get recognized as the big honorary mother of the year.

Alisa turned to Samira, "Why didn't you tell us?"

"I don't ordinarily rat on my friends." She gave Blake a hug.

I was equally reprimanded as Dad scolded earnestly, "I thought better of you Vanessa." It stung. But

I was more of a parent than our parents could or would muster.

"I did it so Blakely could see Tamara." I was honest.

The fact was Blakely barely saw her, so our initiative went unforeseen by the great gods of high school kids. They simply did not respond to our honest ploy to keep two friends together – far from it.

My sister took to her bedroom. She had no note from Chad that day, or that week, or the week after. She called the restaurant which was the only number she had for him, and they said he no longer worked there – he never put that information in a letter and she wondered why not. She was without Tam, her best guy friend in the whole world, and now Chad. It cut like a knife. She had Samira who showed her around Bell, but Blake felt like a black sheep in a herd of muted white. She was used to Stanton despite the sheer humiliation of being hated by the most popular girls in the school. Rumor had it Tamara was hanging with the girls who shamed her the most.

"She tripped me," Blakely had confided to Tamara in the hall after it happened.

But the envelope with the letter was addressed to Chad and Tam read it right there in front of Blakely without saying a word. She recalled the look of suspicion on Tam's face as she said, "How do you know?"

"I felt her boot across my ankle."

Tam walked off without a word.

Blakely didn't work at The Poet's Corner and rarely saw Lacy, Skye, or Cherish after all that had conspired against her. Tamara had classes with Cherish, and Blake wondered if Cherish knew that Tamara knew. It was evident that Tamara was a possessive friend. Blake learned that Tamara was seeing a boy too, and that boy was Joe. Rumor was that Tamara and Joe hooked up as early as Homecoming, but she never said a word to Blakely; Tamara was a hypocrite who saw a boy whilst being a control freak. It was a case of utter jealousy and lascivious behavior similar to Kennedy. Tamara became a snobby girl and Blakely was crushed. Being laughed at by Cherish was an ax in the eye – were they being followers? They still worked at the restaurant and Blakely guessed that the three of them knew too because Tamara told them. It seemed they all stuck together at her expense. She just couldn't work at the place that was so closely connected with Mike's death. She needed an escape from the daily reminders. So, she was a student at Bell and she didn't know at the pep rally whose side she was on or who her friends would be.

"You can sit with us," Samira told her, who was looking at her from the bleachers.

I was her big sister, and I attended the game too but we didn't hang much. She was closer in age to Blake anyway. We got busted forging a note and conspiring to take her to Stanton which did some damage by separating us. Blakely still got rides to school for the year, but Dad

226

only allowed me to drive to school. He otherwise didn't want to see us going out together because we were up to trouble. I let Dad down.

Blake saw the Stanton pep rally from across the way at the bleachers for the away team. They had a parade, floats, and really dressed it up. They were flashy and kind of self-absorbed and she wondered if her place had ever been at Stanton. Bell students were diverse and collective. They didn't fight despite their differences. Blakely liked seeing them get along.

The game began and Jared finally showed with Simone and Billy. They were at the concession stand scoring some snacks and pop. Blakely thought about summer and how her friends worked the concession stands at the resort – she missed them too despite the disintegration of their friendships. She was cold and had heat packs beneath her coat. She wondered how the cheer girls could tolerate the cold despite their earmuffs. She thought about Chad and why he hadn't been writing and why he would have left the restaurant. Blakely barely watched the game and Simone was into chatting about girl stuff, like shades of lipstick and pantyhose that kept her legs warm.

Blake smiled and tried her best to listen, but she was somewhat in a haze. The entire feel of the night was off somehow. Possibly because she was in the mix of a crowd she barely knew and rarely talked about girlish things; she and Tam were into things like sports and parties. Lots of parties. Samira's dad was strict, and Blake was surprised to see her at the game. Sherry and I showed up at the bleachers after getting something hot to drink and some nachos. Diesel and Adam gave us blankets they carried from the Jeep. We sat beside Blakely just as she spotted Tamara across the way, and she wasn't alone; Tamara was with Joe and she was talking with Kennedy. Tamara had traded Blakely's friendship with her very own arch nemesis and Joe put his arm around her shoulder. They looked like a couple. Blakely barely knew what to think and felt both terror and remorse. She had been unfriended. Not only that, she had herself a date and a new best friend – what had Blakely done that was so wrong?

By the time I turned my attention back to Blakely she had already left her seat. She was making her way toward Tamara as Kennedy and her girls swarmed Blakely. It was an ugly sight, and I didn't want to just watch. I told Adam we needed to go over there but he said no way because she needed to do whatever she was doing for herself. Then Kennedy pushed Blakely across the shoulder and was backed by all her friends.

"You have no place here you dirty skank!" Kennedy was out of her mind.

I went over there. I was the only one to help her back to her feet as she was again tripped and made to look foolish.

"Go back to Bell," Eric said as the football team was at the fence line before the start of the game. We were flanked by football jerseys and the cheer squad; all the girls on the Stanton cheer team gave us dirty looks and their boyfriends wanted to smash us. Diesel had also crossed the line that divided Bell from Stanton and Troy Matthews, along with Eric, Jeremy and Chris were closing in on them until Joe, the one with the cape, stepped between them and said, "Any fight now and the game is over."

He was right.

"It's better to walk away then." Adam chided and I took him by the arm.

"Blakely is okay." I was trying to find resolve.

"Let's just watch the game," Joe was really trying.

"Well, she does belong at Bell," Eric sniggered.

"And she's coming back with us," Diesel was a tank and they subtly backed off.

"Then let the game speak for itself," Jeremy knocked Eric's shoulder pad with his helmet and Eric shrugged.

"It's an easy win," he said.

"That's why you've lost twice?" Adam was annoyed.

"You keep antagonizing me and I'll smash your face." Eric thought highly of himself, but Diesel was no chump.

"I'd like to smash you…" he was turning red.

"Easy fellas," Joe stood his ground, "just go back to the bleachers. There's no reason to be here."

Blakely was crushed. Her old life at Stanton was truly over and so was her friendship with Tamara. Before going to the bleachers, she looked for Cherish, Lacy and Skye, who were nowhere in sight and she assumed they must be working. We planned to go to The Poet's Corner after the game for something to eat so we walked casually back to the bleachers as the game started and Stanton had the ball. Stanton wanted to crush Bell and our own cheer squad stood focused and intent to out-cheer their opponents as their rivals spoke jabs as the Bucks were trying to defend a third down at the forty-yard line. Then it happened. The Mustangs crossed the line for a touchdown and began to snigger and sneer in sounds only pigs would enjoy.

"Less like a buck and more like a swine," Troy beckoned from the bench as their coach called for a time out. Our cheer girls kept the faith and sounded confident as a stag. They pressed on. At half time the Mustangs were down by a touchdown. I'd like to say that Bell won but we didn't. The Mustangs had their victory against the Bucks in an assaulting fourteen-point lead. Bell left defeated but hadn't lost their confidence as we went to The Poet's Corner to enjoy chatting over food.

"What is their problem with us?" Samira looked

apathetic.

"They chose to hate Blake." I didn't know why.

"Just to hate somebody?"

"I stuck up for Tamara."

"Your friend? Now she's not?"

"I accidentally gave her a letter."

"Can you explain?"

"The letter was meant for Chad."

It was right then I was about to lose it. Blakely was unfriended over a boy, a boy she liked, and Tamara was a selfish friend and a two-faced one at that.

"And who is Chad?"

She told Samira about meeting Chad and his cousin Sedgwick at the reservoir in Virginia then happenstance occurred, and she found him in Florida.

"Kismet!" Samira was flooded with excitement.

"Kiss… what?" Jared bellowed.

"Kizzz…" Samira reiterated. "It means destiny or fate."

It was destiny. It was fate. And now Blakely was potentially to lose him. How did she even know he was alive? The truth was that she didn't know. She didn't know why he left his job, didn't return her letter, or try to call. She was sullen with angst. She wanted to reach him. She had to idle along somewhat unattached to her existence all the way to Christmas when she did not see Chad. He did not come to her as he had previously said in his letters. Blakely had been surrounded by couples everywhere and had to deal with their long-distance relationship and had to kismet her way through life by placing her future into the hands of something beyond herself. Something more powerful than her strength and abilities could endure at times. Something like the laws of serendipity that she read about. The night wasn't over yet, because as Blakely went to the restroom she was met with the one and only Kennedy McCaide along with Angel, Jessica, Vivian, and Chrissy, in the walkway. They surrounded her.

"We knew we could find you here." Kennedy nearly whispered in a horrific kind of way.

The girls had come from the coffee shop, and they were there to meet Tamara. Blakely could see the back of her head through the glass door.

"So, you found me?" Blakely wasn't fazed.

"Well now you know you no longer have your sweet little farm girl," Kennedy sneered.

The girls laughed. They chided about friendships that go south when one person betrays another person.

232

"How did I betray her?" Blakely was so confused.

"You are a lesbian," Kennedy said as if toying with her.

"We were friends." Blakely really didn't want to be there defending herself.

"No. Stupid. You were more than that and you, well, you obviously backstabbed your bestie…" Kennedy glowered.

"As you call her," Jessica piped in.

"Traitor." Vivian scolded and that ended their feud.

Kennedy pushed past Blakely by ramming her in the shoulder.

Shoulder to shoulder they left, and Blakely once again went numb.

She didn't go into the coffee shop. She let it go.

At Christmas Blakely opened gifts with half a heart but Samira and I got together and did something special for our sister.

Blakely was given a voucher to Florida.

We couldn't think of anything else. We didn't know if it would be a round trip or a one-way ticket so she got a voucher – enough money to cover expenses for a week. Blakely held us both tightly.

"Thank you." And she meant it.

Epilogue

At eighteen years old I signed papers voluntarily as Blakely's guardian. I flew out to Virginia and found her there with a dog. Blakely was fifteen and she adopted a dog from the Shenandoah Shepherd Rescue, Inc. – a large Belgian Malinois with the flair of an intense guard dog she named Atsila meaning "fire" in Creek. It was exactly what Blakely needed, both a companion and someone, something, to guard her heart. We drove back to Florida in Blakely's new ride: a hunter green Jeep she named "Kammie" which was her rendition of Kamama meaning "butterfly" to remind her of a once meaningful friendship. We went Jeeping in Blakely's ride back to Florida where she intended to study Veterinary Science once she graduated. She didn't have to spend another year without us. Instead of having a best friend who was like a sister, she had a sister who was a best friend. In the end she found herself in Florida to find, by way of serendipity, a gorgeous fiancé: a native and an indigenous God in Blakely's eyes, in our eyes, so she'll never be alone again, because as she learned – Tamara wrote a letter. The most deceptive and vicious letter … she told Chad that Blakely had gone by way of suicide after the death of her boyfriend. A boy named Mike. It wouldn't be until the popularity of the internet when Tamara would try to apologize, and Chad had only four words: She's dead to you.

Signed,

Vanessa O'Connor (on behalf of Blakely O' Connor)

In the year 2002

ABOUT THE AUTHOR

Candace Meredith earned her Bachelor of Science degree in English Creative Writing from Frostburg State University in the spring of 2008. Her works of poetry, photography and fiction have appeared in literary journals Bittersweet, The Backbone Mountain Review, The Broadkill Review, In God's Hands/ Writers of Grace, A Flash of Dark, Greensilk Journal, Saltfront, Mojave River Press and Review, Scryptic Magazine, Unlikely Stories Mark V, The Sirens Call, The Great Void, BAM Writes, Foreign Literary, Lion and Lilac Magazine, The Green Shoe Sanctuary Literary Journal, Setu Magazine and various others. Candace lives in Virginia with her son and her daughter, her newborn baby and fiancé. She earned her Master of Science degree in Marketing and Communications from West Virginia University. Candace is the author of various books titled Contemplation: Imagery, sound and Form in Lyricism (a collection of poetry), Losing You (a novella collection), Winter Solstice (book 1 of a 4-book series): The Crone (book 2), The Lady of Brighton (book 3), Summer Solstice (book 4 in progress) and her recently published first children's books A-Hoy Frankie Your Riverboat Captain! And Matilda Gets Adopted.

Made in United States
North Haven, CT
23 November 2022

27155937R00134